PIANOS AND
FLOWERS

ALEXANDER McCALL SMITH

PIANOS AND FLOWERS

*Brief Encounters of the
Romantic Kind*

PANTHEON BOOKS   NEW YORK

Copyright © 2019 by Alexander McCall Smith
Photographs © *The Sunday Times* / News Licensing

All rights reserved. Published in the United States by Pantheon Books,
a division of Penguin Random House LLC, New York. Originally
published in hardcover in Great Britain by Polygon Books, an imprint of
Birlinn Limited, Edinburgh, in 2019.

Pantheon Books and colophon are registered trademarks of
Penguin Random House LLC.

Library of Congress Cataloging-in-Publication Data
Name: McCall Smith, Alexander, [date] author.
Title: Pianos and flowers : brief encounters of the romantic kind /
Alexander McCall Smith.
Description: First United States edition. New York : Pantheon Books, 2020.
Identifiers: LCCN 2019056942 (print). LCCN 2019056943 (ebook).
ISBN 9780593315750 (hardcover). ISBN 9780593315767 (ebook).
Classification: LCC PR6063.C326 A6 2020 (print) | LCC PR6063.C326 (ebook) |
DDC 823/.914—dc23
LC record available at lccn.loc.gov/2019056942
LC ebook record available at lccn.loc.gov/2019056943

www.pantheonbooks.com

Jacket illustration by Iain McIntosh
Jacket design by Emily Mahon

Printed in the United States of America
First United States Edition
9 8 7 6 5 4 3 2 1

This book is for David Purdie

CONTENTS

AUTHOR'S NOTE

When I was asked by *The Sunday Times* to write a number of short stories for the newspaper, I suggested that I should select photographs from their extensive photographic archive and create stories based on what I imagined the pictures depicted. Six of the stories were published in the paper—a few of them are included here, but the rest are new. We do not know, of course, who the people in these photographs were, nor what they were up to. They were almost certainly not doing what I say they are, but that is the joy of looking at photographs in this way: from the tiniest visual clue we can create a whole hinterland of experience—of love, of hope, of simply being human.

A.M.S.
SEPTEMBER 2019

Pianos and Flowers

L OOK AT THE MAN AND WOMAN in the foreground of this photograph. They are walking past the unusual topiary without much more than a glance, seemingly indifferent to whatever it was that the topiarist was striving to portray. The man had muttered "Kandinsky" under his breath, a reference to the apparent similarity of the hedge to the figures seen in the artist's painting; the woman had simply sighed and said nothing. Then the two of them pass out of the photograph, and into the rest of their lives.

Further back are three sisters, standing shoulder to shoulder, with their brother on their right. The other man, standing on his own, on their left (our right) is nothing to do with them and had avoided making eye contact. He was simply there, quite coincidentally, waiting for his wife, who had gone inside the house to retrieve her sun hat. When she returned a few minutes after this photograph was taken, they made their way into the rose garden, which cannot be seen here, but which lay off to the right, hidden by the high yew hedge behind the small groups of strollers.

We do not know who that couple was, although one of the sisters later remarked, "That man in the garden was Dutch, I think. I may be wrong, but I think he looked Dutch." Another said, "How can you tell?" To which the reply came, "I don't know. There are some things that you just feel to be the case. You can't be sure, but you think it. It's hard to explain, actually." And the third said, "Intuition. That's the word you're looking for. Intuition." As it happened, he was not Dutch, but Belgian—the director of a company that imported rubber from what was then known as the Belgian Congo. His grandchildren would say of this involvement, "Don't look at us, we had nothing to do with it," although what they had read about the Congo and Leopold's doings there made them shudder with embarrassment and regret.

The three women remained, as did the man accompanying them. They stood there for at least twenty minutes, and then, as if discouraged, they went back inside the house and had tea there rather than in the garden, like most of the guests.

Who were they? Why did they stand in a straight line? What did they expect, or want? Are they still alive? Each of these questions can be answered, but the last one, the question that an old photograph so often raises, might be answered first. The age of the photograph, usually revealed by the clothing, may settle the survival issue. We may guess at a decade: skirt length, hats, the presence or absence of gloves—these may be clues enough. And, the question of survival having been settled, we may turn our thoughts to how the people in the photograph met their end. In this case, one of the women was killed in a traffic accident in Bristol. Another died in 1956, of rapidly progressing septicaemia. The third lived to see the fall of the Berlin Wall. The man died at sixty-two, having fallen overboard in a yachting accident on the Solent; a spinnaker, badly handled, had folded in upon itself, wrapping him in its embrace and eventually pushing him off the deck into the sea. He was a strong swimmer, but it is thought that cold-water shock took its toll.

None of these siblings did anything out of the ordinary with their lives. People may be remembered by the things they made, or the things they made happen, perhaps by their sayings, their acts of creation, however modest. None of these four left anything much behind them. Obscurity is quick, and tactful; it keeps a straight face if it overhears our hopes of being remembered, but it knows better. So, in a sense, it was as if these four had never existed. Some lives are like that— they leave little trace, as unrecorded as were those countless lives led before writing and photography gave some degree of permanence to our human experience.

He was called Thomas Sanderson, and his sisters were Annette, Flora, and Stephanie. Thomas was two years older than Annette, who was the senior of the sisters, in turn two years the senior of Flora, who was born two years before Stephanie. "We are a perfectly spaced family," Annette was fond of saying, "even if our poor brother is somewhat outnumbered by his sisters."

"I don't mind that at all," said Thomas. "In fact, I consider myself lucky to have three sisters. That is great good fortune in this life."

"It's very nice of you to say that," said Flora. "And we're very fortunate to have such a dear brother."

They are pictured here in England, where they lived for most of their lives. Their early childhood, though, had been spent in Penang, in what was then the Straits Settlements. Their father, Robert, the head of a port warehousing firm in George Town, also owned a small rubber estate in one of the neighbouring Malayan states. He had no taste for the jungle, though, and left the management of the estate to a taciturn Glaswegian, who had five children by a Malay woman. Robert's wife, Francie, disliked the Glaswegian, being scandalised by his casual fathering of his brood of children. None of the children had been brought up to speak English; none wore shoes; and the two small boys amongst them had long hair that their mother lovingly tied in a ponytail. They were, without exception, very happy in their freedom, and indifferent to Francie's frosty disapproval on the rare occasions that she visited the estate with her husband.

Francie disapproved of many things. Like many women in colonial society, she was acutely aware of her status, which, by the nature of things at the time, was entirely dependent on her husband's position. Robert was well off and had been in George Town for a long time, unlike some of the more recent arrivals, whom the older planters and traders looked down upon. He was on the committee of the local Chamber of Commerce, which gave him a certain amount of clout and which ensured invitations to official functions, even if he and Francie were rarely placed at the top table at a government dinner. He had also been the Vice-Chairman of the Club for a double term of office, and that, again, conferred some standing. But for most purposes he was outranked by senior government officers and, more significantly perhaps, had an air about him that aroused the suspicions of the more snobbish. These people were discreet about it, and would not openly question his credentials, but privately they made remarks about the fact that his hair was parted in the middle, and that his shoes were not quite what one might expect. "They like shoes like that in Shanghai," one of the members of the Club said, and laughed. "Not that I'm saying they're not well made—they are. Frightfully elegant and all that, but, you know . . ."

In George Town the family lived in a large house on the slope of the hill. This had verandas that ran around all four sides, both on the ground floor and on the storey above. These had screens that could be unrolled to keep out mosquitoes, and were furnished with teak planters' chairs. There were elephant feet cut to form the base of brass-topped side tables, and on the floor there were mats made from thin strips of rattan. Ceiling fans rotated slowly, disturbing the languid air only enough to give slight relief from the heat and humidity. "Our fans provide purely psychological relief," Robert was fond of saying.

The children loved playing on these verandas, sending chipped carpet bowls shooting from one end to another, and dragging one another about on the mats, as if they were sledges. The smooth cement floor, polished red, was tended by a servant who spent half of his waking hours bringing a shine to the surface. His hands were dyed red by the polish, and the knees of his khaki trousers were permanently the same colour. He was a Tamil, who lived in the servants' block in the back yard. He had a slight limp, which came from some childhood injury, and a ready smile. He worshipped Robert for reasons that were obscure, although there was a story about Robert having done something about a debt that the Tamil had inherited and that would otherwise have burdened him for life. "A trifling sum," said Robert, "but you know what it's like for these people." Francie said, "Yes, but you have to be careful not to spoil them. You'll get no thanks if you spoil them, you know."

Francie had always known that her time in Penang was finite. She employed a tutor for the children, and there was a small school where people sent their children until the age of ten, but after that there was no option but to send them home. Home, of course, was England, a country that the children had visited a few times when Robert took long leave, but that was nevertheless a strange and rather romantic place to them. England was the backdrop for their history lessons, and for the books they read; it was the place where the King lived, where knights jousted at tournaments, where people lived in castles and country houses; it was a place where there were never any storms, or cooking smells, or poisonous snakes. And yet, in spite of that, it was a place where you went off to boarding school and had to sleep in dormitories and be careful not to offend the prefects placed in authority over you.

Francie knew that once she started a family, in a few years she would have to take the children home and get them settled. Some people had arrangements with relatives, who would look after children during the school holidays; she was not too sure about that. She had heard too many stories of children being miserable because the people looking after them were doing it only for the money, or out of a sense of duty, rather than any enthusiasm for the children themselves. Neither she nor Robert had anybody whom she felt they could trust, and so she would have to stay in England, while Robert lived by himself in Penang. That sort of solution was never entirely satisfactory; so many men could not cope with loneliness, and gave in to temptation, no matter how firm their resolve at the beginning. She had known of at least two women whose husbands had behaved that way when left in the East by their wives. One had taken up with a local woman; another had had a florid and public affair with the wife of a senior government official, bringing about disgrace and unhappiness in more or less equal measure.

In Penang, there were few constraints on the children's freedom. The house had four acres of garden, presided over by an ancient Chinese gardener and his young Malay assistant. This gardener was fascinated by the children. They seemed so strange to him, so exotic, rather like rare plants. He created paths through the undergrowth for them to run along, and built them a treehouse in a flowering Malaysian blackwood. There was a large pond for which the gardener's assistant had made a raft for the children to use. On this raft there was a small cabin on which the gardener had inscribed Chinese characters in green paint. "Good luck," he said, his grin revealing a few well-worn teeth as he pointed to the characters. "That is good luck. Chinese. Plenty of good luck." The children nodded; they thought of the Chinese language as being composed of pithy appeals to fortune: *good luck, happy fate, happiness, much money,* and so on, while Malay, of which they had picked up a smattering, seemed full of domestic commands, *wash, put away, polish.*

The house next door was invisible from the Sanderson property, being shielded from view by the thickness of the garden vegetation. This house was even larger than theirs, a fact that irritated Francie, as it was occupied by a Chinese family with whom she would not mix socially. This family, the Fongs, had two daughters who were roughly of an age with Annette and Flora. These girls had learned English at the convent that they attended, the Fongs being Catholic and prominent supporters of Catholic missions in Manchuria. This philanthropy was, some time later, to prove their undoing in an unexpected and harrowing way.

The Fong girls engaged in imaginative games, the narrative of which the Sanderson girls found hard to follow. Roles and names were solemnly allocated, almost always in Chinese, with the occasional concession being made to English. The games were complex, although some were recognised by the Sanderson girls as being loosely based on the story portrayed on willow-pattern plates. These involved hiding, being found, running away, being caught—all accompanied by breathless commentary from the Fong girls. Others were pure invention. "A very sad girl lived in a house with a father who had a dragon," intoned one of the Fongs. "This sad girl said she would run away with her friend, who was not sad. They took the dragon with them. They had many adventures. The dragon ate a wicked nun." That, of course, was a reference to the convent the Fongs attended.

When they tired of these games, the Sandersons would take the Fongs into the kitchen and plead for lemonade. If they spotted Thomas, the Fong girls would giggle amongst themselves, shooting glances at him and then covering their mouths with a hand to conceal their giggling.

"What's wrong with those stupid girls?" Thomas asked his sisters. "Are they on laughing gas?"

"They think you're funny," said Annette.

"They think all boys are funny," Flora said.

Thomas rolled his eyes. "They don't know anything."

Occasionally the Fong girls invited Annette and Flora to their house. They taught them Mah Jong, although this tested their patience as teachers. It seemed inexplicable to them that anybody would not know of the significance of the wind or dragon tiles. Were English girls really that ignorant? Were they like that in England itself—unaware of basic things, such as the rules of Mah Jong? Surely not.

The Fong girls had Chinese names but used Western names, Cecilia and Joan, at the convent and when with non-Chinese people. They were learning the piano, and had an Italian piano teacher who came to the house three times a week. He gave them each a piece of chocolate if their playing demonstrated conscientious practising; if they fell below the standard expected, they were treated to a sad shaking of the head and a wagging of the teacher's well-manicured finger. It was the same finger that he used in place of a metronome when listening to the girls' playing.

Joan Fong loved flowers. While Cecilia, who was the better musician, played the piano and Annette and Flora listened from the Fongs' gold-coloured sofa, Joan would arrange flowers that she had picked earlier that day from their garden. She would sometimes present Cecilia with a bouquet of flowers at the end of the piece, and Cecilia would lower herself from the piano stool, bowing deeply in the direction of her audience.

She would lay the flowers on the piano keyboard and bow once again, this time to an imaginary audience beyond the heads of the Sanderson girls.

"See?" said Joan. "One day Cecilia will be very, very famous. In England. See?"

Penang, the Chinese gardener, the world of the Fongs, the piano, the flowers—all these seemed so far away once they went home. "But this isn't home," complained Annette. "Home is our house . . ." By which she meant the house on the hill, with its polished red floors and verandas; not this neat box of a house in Budleigh Salterton, with its heavy curtains and stifling respectability. "Many people," said Francie, "would be more than pleased to live in Budleigh Salterton." She said that, though, partly in an effort to convince herself that she should be one of them—one of those who aspired to Budleigh Salterton—whereas she really found it stultifying. She missed the ladies' nights at the Club; she missed the tea parties where she was able to condescend to the wives of junior officials; she even missed the things of which she disapproved. Disapproval may provide as much a *raison d'être* as wholehearted endorsement; who amongst us does not enjoy at least some of our animosities? Everything here seemed too *lodged,* too firmly fixed in its place to offer any excitement. And what lay before her but year after lonely year of this separation from her husband, of writing a weekly letter in which she tried to summon up enough novelty to last a page or two before she reached the concluding line, *I miss you terribly.* That was true enough; she did miss him. And he her? She hoped so, and wrote to a close friend in Penang to ask her. *Do you think he's missing me a lot?* And the friend replied, *Darling, I saw him two days ago at the Club, and you know what he talked about? You. All the time. Nothing else. That answers your question, don't you think?*

The children were sent off to boarding schools, although the youngest was kept at home for a year or two after arrival in England. But when Stephanie joined her sisters at school, Francie was left by herself in the house for long periods until the girls had an exeat weekend or the term came to an end. She became proficient at crossword puzzles, for which she had a hitherto undetected talent, and became a much stronger bridge player than she had been in Penang. She read constantly, almost a novel a day. She devoured Maugham's *The Casuarina Tree,* saying to herself, *Yes, yes, that's exactly right,* although her friend wrote to her from Penang to say how angry they were that he had abused their hospitality by writing about them. *That man,* she steamed, *accepted the hospitality of a whole lot of people—some of whom you and I actually know, Francie—and then writes about them like that! As if adultery and back-biting were the only things we thought about from the moment we get out of bed—rarely our own bed, in Mr. Maugham's view—until the time we turn the lights out. If you could hear some of the things they're saying about that man here, and his so-called secretary . . .* The invective made her briefly homesick, and she went back to one or two of the stories, allowing nostalgia to overcome her, and thought of the gardener and his boy, and of her husband in his office at the warehouse, under the fans, and those invoices that they stuck on spikes mounted on wooden bases, and the Chinese clerks at their desks.

Thomas was sent to a school that prided itself on its academic standards, and thrived there. He had his father's head for figures, and would in due course be a businessman like him—perhaps take over the warehouses. The girls were sent to a school that was distinctly less enthusiastic about academic matters. Their brochure spoke of the goal of the well-rounded young woman, "able to hold her own in any sort of company and competent in both the domestic and sporting fields." This statement was accompanied by pictures of several teenage girls, one holding a test tube up to the light and another in the process of committing a baking tin to an oven; a third girl was poised to dive from a high diving board, while watched by several admiring younger girls below.

The girls were happy enough at this school. They liked their teachers, who tended to be people who had failed in careers elsewhere or had chosen to come to the school because they had heard that it was generally undemanding. Some of the teachers were part-time, as was Captain Edmunds, who taught horse-riding. He spent three afternoons a week at the school and all of Saturday, and his lessons were always well subscribed. He was just a little bit too old—he was forty—to be of interest to the senior girls, but he was much admired by the geography teacher, Miss Littlewood, who watched him from the window of her room in one of the school boarding houses. The girls had not taken long to work out why Miss Littlewood appeared at the window so regularly, standing just far enough back so that Captain Edmunds would not see her if he looked up from the dressage ring.

Annette came up with the idea of writing a note purporting to be from Captain Edmunds. It would suggest a meeting that evening in the tack-room at the school stables. *My dear Angela,* she wrote, *I know that we've scarcely met, and I hope you don't think it forward of me to suggest that we meet this evening in the tack-room. I have some work to do on the saddles and would much appreciate a chance to get to know you a bit better. 6 p.m. Until then, John Edmunds (Captain).*

"Perfect," said the friend to whom she showed the note. "And to him? What does she say to him?"

Annette produced another note. *My dear Captain Edmunds, Would it be possible for us to meet in the tack-room at 6 p.m. this evening? There is something I would dearly love to talk to you about, but feel that it will be better to have this conversation in private. Cordially yours, Angela Littlewood, B.A.*

"Brilliant," said the friend. "But do you think it will work?"

"Yes," said Annette. "In two months I bet they'll be engaged."

The notes were dispatched, the one to Captain Edmunds being left on the seat of his BSA motorcycle; the other being placed in Miss Littlewood's pigeonhole outside the staff common room. Just before 6 p.m. Annette saw Captain Edmunds making his way towards the tack-room. Five minutes later, Miss Littlewood was seen adopting a slightly circuitous route to the same destination.

"You see!" crowed Annette. "It worked like a charm."

At the beginning of 1938 Robert wrote to Francie: *I can't tell you how worried I am about Japan. Manchuria is just a beginning, you know—they'll be coming after us at the first opportunity. We have the R.A.F. at Butterworth, but a chap I know says their planes are no match to what the Japs have. And there aren't very many of them. And what are Chamberlain and others doing back home? Saying we mustn't upset Germany too much. Well, I can tell you, it's not just Germany—it's the Japanese too. Do you know what they did when they took Nanjing? They murdered— yes, murdered—hundreds of thousands of people. Nobody knows how many, because virtually anybody who saw what was going on was disposed of. I bumped into Fong the other day in the street and the poor fellow was in a bad way. He's been doing a lot for the China Relief Fund—we had a benefit for them at the Club the other day. Fong says he saw pictures of the Japs using live Chinese prisoners for bayonet practice. He started to blub, he was so upset—and who can blame him? It's different for us— nobody's using us for bayonet practice—just yet. I'm immensely relieved, Francie, that we got you and the children out of here. I don't think they'll dare come here just yet—and they'll never take Singapore—but it's very worrying nonetheless.*

Robert remained in Penang after the outbreak of war in Europe. In 1941, Penang fell to the Japanese. At Butterworth, the Royal Air Force's planes were quickly destroyed, and there was unopposed bombing of George Town. The British effectively threw in the towel, to the surprise of those who had considered them invincible. Penang had been described as a fortress; it proved anything but. The British had at least planned their retreat, evacuating the European population of the island before the Japanese arrived, which meant that Robert found himself in Singapore, with only two suitcases of clothing and possessions. His money, at least, was safe, and he took a room in the Tanglin Club, writing to tell Francie that he was comfortable and would be working with a friend who owned a number of go-downs. *We'll be all right, I suspect, as this place is going to be a harder nut to crack. Don't worry. They'll never make it down this far.* He signed up as acting paymaster for a regiment that had lost a number of its officers further north. He was given the temporary rank of Captain Sanderson, and was popular with the men for his liberal view of allowance issues.

One evening on the street outside Raffles he saw a man whom he had known slightly in Penang—a Chinese merchant who had run an import-export business. They greeted one another like old friends.

"It is very bad," said the merchant, his voice faltering as he spoke. "They are killing us, you know. This Sook Ching business. Killing Chinese—just because we're Chinese. They say it's because they think we are anti-Japanese and that we're a threat. But they are killing anybody and everybody. And a man with tattoos—he gets it, because they think if you have tattoos you are a gangster. And all our big men, too, our leaders, they're killing them because they are prominent citizens and they fear them. And our women—comfort women they call them. They are taking them too. We thought the British would protect us. I do not like to speak about that, because my heart is too heavy, Mr. Sanderson."

Robert listened, appalled. There were whispers and rumours; there were even reports in the press. But these urgent, harrowing words spoken by one such as this merchant were of a different order.

"Tell me, Mr. Chao—Edward Fong, did you know him?"

The merchant looked away. "I am very sorry, Mr. Sanderson, but Edward Fong had helped the China Relief Fund. There had been pictures of him presenting cheques to the Fund. The Japanese can read. It was not good for Fong."

It took Robert a few moments to gather his thoughts. "And his girls—well, young women by now, of course. Any news of them?"

From the look in the merchant's eyes, he could tell what the answer would be. And so he said, "I mustn't ask you to speak about things you do not want to speak about. I must not."

"Thank you," said the merchant. He looked up at the sky. "There is rain coming. I must get inside."

Robert was taken prisoner after Singapore fell. He survived for almost a year, before dying of dysentery. Francie did not hear of his death for ten months, when the news was passed on to her from Australia. She had feared this from the moment she had heard he had been taken prisoner; she had done much of her grieving. She stayed on in the house at Budleigh Salterton, although she often went to spend time with her sister in London. She became ill, although her doctor found it difficult to diagnose the cause. She went off her food and her health deteriorated. It seemed to her friends that she had lost the will to live. "We're not giving up," they said. "You mustn't."

She knew they were right. It was no good being defeatist, and she made an effort with war work. But she felt that there was little point in carrying on. She had done everything she needed to do: she had raised four children and launched them. She had made the most of her marriage. She had played the cards she had been dealt without complaint. She felt that was enough. Her final illness was a blessing, she thought. They did not tell her what it was, but she felt it within her, a gnawing feeling that seemed to be taking over. She would not fight it—what point was there?

After the war, with both parents dead, Thomas felt that he was responsible for his sisters. He was now a shipping agent in London with a successful and growing business. His sisters, none of whom was married, lived in a house three doors away—a house that he paid for and kept in good repair. Thomas himself lived with Vinnie, a young woman whom he described as his housekeeper, but who was too well spoken for that to convince anybody. She was his mistress. She was Catholic and on principle would not divorce her husband, a philanderer called Ted Barber, to whom she had been married for only six months. It was better, she thought, to live with Thomas than to risk eternal damnation by bringing her marriage to an end. God, she imagined, would be understanding, and would appreciate the effort she had made to uphold the Church's precepts, even if her relationship with Thomas could not be regularised.

Thomas saw it as his duty to look after his sisters, none of whom had acquired any skills that would enable her to get a job. Their father had left enough money in his estate to ensure that none of them was indigent. But although parents might make provision for the material needs of their offspring, they cannot, in modern conditions, find spouses for them. That, Thomas realised, was now his responsibility as their brother.

"It would be nice if you met somebody," he said. "I'm not saying you *have* to. I'm just saying it would be nice—that's all."

The sisters looked at one another.

"Yes," said Annette. She, as the oldest of the three, tended to be the spokesman. "Yes, it would be nice, but how are we going to do that, might I ask? We don't know any men, really." She turned to Flora. "Do you know any suitable men, Flora?"

Flora shook her head. "There are hardly any men around," she said.

Stephanie sighed. "It would be much easier, I think, if we had a tennis court. Like the one we had in Budleigh Salterton. We could invite men to come and play tennis . . ."

"And then marry them," interjected Flora.

"You may laugh," said Stephanie. "But it's true. People with tennis courts have very active social lives. Everybody knows that."

"But we don't have one," Annette said. "And we don't even know where it used to be."

"Behind the garage," suggested Flora. "There's that flat bit there, and I think that was the tennis court."

Thomas smiled. "I don't think it helps to argue about

where the tennis court used to be. Far better to think of ways of introducing you to men." He paused. "We could have a party, of course. Or . . ." He had remembered something, and the sisters watched him closely. "Or I could take you to something I've been invited to. They—the hosts—don't know about Vinnie, and anyway, she doesn't like garden parties and so wouldn't come."

The sisters expressed interest, and the decision was taken. Thomas knew the hosts well and could easily ask them if he could bring his three sisters with him. What was more, he would buy each of them a new dress for the occasion. "You can choose whatever you like," he said. "People will be dressing up, I imagine."

The four of them went to the garden party and stood for some time, in a line, on the lawn. One or two people smiled at them in a friendly fashion as they walked past, and one, an elderly man with a drinker's complexion, raised his hat and said, "Fine day for a garden party, isn't it?" That was all. Nobody else paid them any attention, and certainly any single men, if there were any invited, were not in evidence. After drinking tea inside the house, they all left, in silence.

Thomas was apologetic. "That was a thoroughly useless party," he said. "Frankly, I don't know why people bother to throw parties like that."

Flora agreed. "Worse than useless," she said. "But we're not blaming you, Tommy."

Then, in his ship-broking office, Thomas heard of a party being held by a group of naval officers whose ship was in harbour. "I've had this invitation to a party," he said to his sisters.

"They very kindly said I could bring other people with me if I wanted to. They're naval officers."

Stephanie perked up. "Sailors?" she asked.

"Yes," replied Thomas. "Officers—not Jack Tars."

"Let's go," said Stephanie. "You never know."

Thomas remembered the unsuccessful garden party. He had an idea. "Why don't you girls dress up in naval outfits? You know what I mean—nice white outfits with a blue scarf and an anchor motif on the sleeves, maybe. Something like that."

Annette thought this a good suggestion, as did Flora and Stephanie. "I think Tommy's idea is really wonderful," she enthused. "Let's do it."

They had two weeks to prepare their outfits, and then they were ready. "You look stunning," said Thomas. "They'll love that."

They went to the party. The sailors were generous hosts. Junior ratings, in smart white outfits, handed drinks around. The sisters' outfits were a real success, and they were soon surrounded by three young officers, who talked to them in an animated and clearly interested fashion.

From the other side of the room, Thomas observed the scene with satisfaction. At his side was Vinnie.

"Look at that," said Thomas. "Success at last."

Vinnie was not so sure. "Why should those young men be so interested in girls dressed up as sailors?" she asked.

Thomas frowned.

"Just asking," said Vinnie. "That's all."

———

It was Annette who married one of the naval officers. Thomas said to her, "You do know what you're doing, don't you? Being married to a sailor means he'll be away for long periods. You know that, don't you?" She did, but she was sure it would not matter. "Look at Mummy," she said. "Look at how long she and Daddy were separated. She was happy enough, don't you think?" Thomas just looked at her.

But it was a good marriage, and she had three sons and a daughter. Her husband was given a shore job, and he remained in that for most of his career. She pre-deceased him by five years. Flora married an engineer who worked for a firm of instrument makers. "Nothing happened in my life," she once said to Annette. "Nothing." Stephanie was engaged, briefly, but discovered her fiancé was a compulsive gambler and brought the engagement to an end. She never married, but she bought a small hotel that she ran by herself for over forty years. There was a piano in the dining room of this hotel— a piano that was never played—and occasionally she would stop by it and depress one of the keys and remember Cecilia Fong. And she would turn round, to an empty room, and hold out a hand for the presentation of flowers.

Look again at the photograph, at the man and woman in the foreground. That was Captain Edmunds and Angela Littlewood.

I'd Cry Buckets

T HE SWEEP OF THE HILLS. The burn tumbling joyously across the rock. The pony sure-footed but scared of moving water, picking his way gingerly under the burden of the dead stag. And the two boys, who were sixteen, and who were tired from being up on the hill since six that morning when it was still chill and misty and not quite yet light. They had two uncomfortable hours to go before they would be back at the lodge; walking downhill could be as demanding as climbing—different muscles were involved, and these might not be in such good order as those used when ascending.

"Are you all right?"

That was Bruce, the boy in the front, the one leading the pony.

David replied, "Yes, I'm all right."

Bruce said, "I made myself really stiff last year. I wasn't used to walking downhill, you see, and by the time I got down I could hardly walk, I'm telling you. My knees seemed to have locked."

David said nothing. He had noticed the blood that had dripped across the pony's flanks. The pony must be used to it, as animals could panic when they smelled blood—or so he had read somewhere. Or was that only when the blood they smelled was their own? Perhaps that was it.

Bruce said, "This burn has a name, but I always forget what it is. It's in Gaelic. We had a keeper who spoke Gaelic. He knew all the names and what they meant. Often they're very simple. The big glen. The small burn. That sort of thing. All in Gaelic. This is called the white glen, you know."

David looked up to where the hills reached the sky. "Why the white glen?"

"Because of the light. It just looks white. You often see a layer of cloud halfway up the hill. It moves across like a white line. I think that may be the reason."

The pony hesitated, but then continued.

"Come on, Billy," urged Bruce, tugging at the rein. "You're doing well. Come on."

"Do animals ever think they're going to die?" David asked.

Bruce shook his head. "I don't think so. They want to avoid being hurt, I suppose. They're frightened of that. But they don't know about actually dying, I'd say. They don't understand they won't go on forever."

"And is that better, do you think?"

Bruce shrugged. "Probably. Knowing something can be hard. Sometimes it's best not to know." He glanced at his friend. "Do you want to stop? We could rest, if you like."

David shook his head. He wanted to get down to the house. He was thirsty but did not want to drink from one of the burns because people said you could get ill that way.

"No, let's carry on."

"They'll have something ready for us when we get down," said Bruce. "Sandwiches. A bottle of beer."

"Are you allowed? I mean, do your parents let you?" There was envy in David's voice.

"Yes, they said that when I turned sixteen I could. Only

beer, though. Which doesn't worry me—I can't stand whisky. Can you?"

"The smell's too strong. It's like that stuff you use for model aeroplanes."

"Dope? To make the paper tight?"

"Yes."

Bruce patted the pony's nose. "It's so soft," he said. "A pony has a soft nose. Like very supple leather. Something like that."

They continued to walk, moving down the contour lines until the house came into sight, ringed by the trees that had been so conspicuously absent on the bare, higher ground. The pony was left at the steading, handed over to a man who took charge of it and its burden, the finished stag.

"Good work," he said. "Good work, lads."

"They'll put the stag in the deer larder," Bruce explained. "Over there. See that building? That's the deer larder. There are big hooks. Do you want to see?"

David shook his head. He did not want to look at the stag, with its still-open eyes and its useless legs. "No. No thanks."

"Well, in that case we can go back to the house. We can get out of these wet things." There had been rain—not heavy, but intermittent and almost imperceptible, in the way of Highland rain. Now their tweeds—lent them by the keeper from a store of clothing—were damp, weighty with the moisture of the air.

Bruce's parents were in the house, along with several guests. Tea was being served in a drawing room, and the adults crooned compliments: *The conquering heroes return; our dinner is secured; Dick Dead-Eye and his friend, no less.* Bruce smiled wanly, glancing at David, as if to apologise. Parents are inexplicably embarrassing to sixteen-year-olds—they always have been.

"Who took the shot?" Bruce's father asked.

"I did," said Bruce.

"And you didn't have a stalker with you!" marvelled one of the guests. "I'd never manage."

"He knows his way round," said Bruce's father proudly.

"Always has," added his mother.

They drank a cup of tea and then left the room. Dinner would be in two hours, they were told. They should wear their kilts, with black tie. David would find the things he needed laid out on his bed. He had brought his kilt but did not have the black jacket and tie. Again the clothing store would come to his rescue.

"Is it always like this?" he asked Bruce.

"Like what?"

"Like a sort of hotel."

Bruce nodded. "Mostly. When we have guests in the stalking season, that is."

"Who are they?"

This was answered with a shrug. "Friends of my parents. That thin chap with the glasses runs a shipyard down in Glasgow. My father sells him steel."

"I see."

Bruce looked at him. "Come and keep me company."

"I need to change. And I need to take a bath."

"You've got plenty of time," said Bruce. "Come when you've changed. My room's down there, at the end."

After his bath and his change into the kilt, David made his way to Bruce's room. The door was ajar, but he knocked and waited until he was invited in. Bruce was sitting on the edge of the bed, struggling with a cuff link.

"Could you do this for me?" he asked. "If you don't get these things in before you put your shirt on, it can take hours."

He helped push the reluctant cuff link through the buttonhole. He noticed that it was inscribed with initials.

"My grandfather's," Bruce explained. "I've got all his engraved stuff because my initials are the same as his." He pointed to a chair. "You can sit down over there. That chair. Talk to me."

He did not know what to say.

"Go on," Bruce repeated. "Talk to me. Surely you've got something to say. Tell me about South America."

"I know nothing about South America. I've never been there."

Bruce laughed. "Neither have I. But talk to me about where we'll go—you and I—when we go off to South America."

"Are we going?"

"Why not? I'm fed up with school. Aren't you? We can go to . . . to Colombia, perhaps. Or Peru."

"I'd like that, I suppose."

"So would I," said Bruce. "And the Andes. We'd see the Andes."

He entered into the spirit of it. "Of course. You wouldn't want to go to South America without seeing the Andes."

"No."

There was a brief silence. Bruce said something that David did not hear.

"What was that?"

"University. I said university."

"What about it?" David asked.

"Have you decided?"

David sighed. "I'm trying to. I know we've got a bit of time . . ."

"Not much."

"No, not much. But I suppose we can still change our minds without anybody going off at the deep end about it." David paused. "They keep saying 'make up your mind'—not just about this, but about a lot of things. But what they're really trying to do is to make up your mind *for you*."

Bruce laughed. "Yes. I know exactly what you mean."

David thought of the conversation with his English teacher, who talked to him, constantly it seemed, about the Oxford college he called "The House." "You must go there, David," the teacher said. "It's the obvious place for you." But it was not explained to him why this was the case, although he thought it was something to do with the fact that his teacher had been a contemporary there of a highly regarded poet. *Wystan said this, Wystan said that*—they mocked him for his enthusiasm.

Bruce interrupted his train of thought. "St. Andrews," he said.

"You've decided?" asked David. "St. Andrews?"

"Yes. My father wants me to go there. He's not putting it that bluntly, but I can tell that he'll . . . he'll die if I went somewhere else. Particularly England. No, not really. But he really wants me to because he was there himself. He said he'd buy me a car if I go there."

David drew in his breath. A car. And felt a pang of envy, which he knew was wrong. He had been brought up to believe that you were never envious of the good fortune of others. And yet, why was envy so bad if it was so natural a feeling? Most of our feelings had some point to them, surely; we fell in love because we needed to keep the species going; we felt angry when provoked because we needed to protect ourselves; we felt disgust over things that smelled rotten because if we did not, and ate them, then we might die. It was all very natural.

He looked at his friend, and then looked away. Why did we feel friendship for others? What was the point of it? Loneliness, perhaps. We did not like to be by ourselves too much. Yes, friendship was important for that reason, but there must be others. There must be something that converted the feeling into something noble, something that you might want to paint or write a poem about. But he was not sure about what it was that made things that important; perhaps if he went to "The House" he would be admitted to that secret, whatever it was.

"You wouldn't think of coming to St. Andrews?" Bruce suddenly asked. "With me?"

He said the first thing that came into his mind. "I never considered it."

"Apparently, it's a great place. There's something called the Kate Kennedy. They have a procession . . ."

David tossed his head back. "You don't swallow all that, do you? Come on, Bruce."

Bruce looked disappointed. "I'm not saying that all tradition's a good thing. Some, though."

"I don't believe in any of that. Sorry. And, anyway, do you really need a car?"

David regretted the question the moment he had posed it. It was cutting, and snide, and he did not wish to hurt his friend. It was envy, he thought, that had prompted him to talk about the car that way. If anybody had offered *him* a car, he would have accepted with alacrity. We belittle the things we secretly want ourselves. He remembered somebody telling him that, but he could not remember who it was. "I'm sorry," he said. "I didn't mean to sound like that."

But Bruce had not taken offence. "Like what? Sound like what?"

"Forget it. Nothing."

"I suppose we'd better go down for dinner," said Bruce. "Have you got everything you need?"

He had.

"Then I'll see you at seven. They like us to be punctual. My dad in particular is keen on that. He says that punctuality is the greatest of the virtues. He can even say that in Latin."

David thought: He has a father who can say things in Latin. He has this place. He has his own rifle.

Later, going back to his room after collecting his watch from the bathroom, where he had inadvertently left it, he heard voices coming from behind the door of Bruce's room. Something made him slow down, then stop.

". . . anyway, how well do you know him?"

That was Bruce's father.

"Pretty well. He's in my house at school. Same year."

There was a short silence. Then, "You say you don't think he likes stalking?"

"No. I don't think he does."

The father again. "There's something about him I'm not quite sure of. Is he one of those boys, do you think? I don't want you associating with that sort of boy."

David felt his heart beat fast within him.

"No, of course not."

"You understand what I'm talking about?"

"Yes. Of course I do."

"Good."

David moved away, the back of his neck hot with shame. Did Bruce's father not see it? So he thought that of him. That's what he thought, and all the time he should be looking at Bruce. Or not. How could you tell?

He tried to put the overheard conversation out of his mind. At the dinner table, he sat next to the wife of the thin man who ran a shipyard. She talked to him about books she had read. Had he tried Buchan? He really should. There was something for everybody in Buchan. And she liked poetry too; she liked Wilfred Owen and Walter de la Mare. And Benson. He was very funny, Benson. He should certainly try Benson.

He looked at Bruce's father, who smiled at him, as if he had said nothing. He looked away.

At ten o'clock he and Bruce left the party. In the corridor, Bruce said, "I don't think you enjoyed this evening, did you?"

He looked down at the floor.

"Or the stalking?" Bruce continued.

He shook his head.

There was silence. Then Bruce said, "Neither did I."

"Why?"

"I felt sorry for the stag. You may think that odd—because I shot it—but I felt sorry. They made me do it."

"Them—your parents?"

"Yes."

And suddenly Bruce reached out and put his hand on his shoulder. "Could we go and see it?" he asked.

David nodded. "If you want to."

"I do."

They went out into the darkness. Outside the deer larder door there was a light switch. A dim bulb was illuminated within.

They saw the stag, hung up on its hook. Underneath it, on the concrete floor, was a small dark pool of blood.

Bruce stepped forward. He touched the animal's coat. Then, drawing closer, he pressed its flank. The carcase moved slightly. "Sorry," he said. "Sorry, sorry, sorry."

He turned to face David. "I'm so ashamed," he said. "I'm so ashamed of this . . ." He gestured behind him, to the stag.

"No," said David. "Don't be."

"And of myself. I'm ashamed of myself."

"Because . . ."

"Because of things I can't tell you about."

David hesitated. "But what if I were to tell you that I already knew. And that it doesn't matter. Nothing like that matters, you know. It's not a big thing."

Bruce stared at him. "You're kind," he said.

They left the deer larder and made their way back to the house. There was still a glow of light in the sky, as they were in the far north, where it stayed light almost until midnight. David shivered, although the summer air was warm. "That smell," he said. "That coconut smell."

"Gorse bushes," said Bruce. "The flowers smell just like coconut."

"And that sound?" asked David.

"That's the waterfall. The burn behind the house has a waterfall. We could go and see it if you like."

David shook his head. "I think I should turn in."

Inside, they said goodnight, and David returned to his room, which was at the end of a long and dimly lit corridor. On the walls there were engravings of Blackface sheep—portraits of champions. There was an oil painting of a man launching a boat on a Highland loch.

He lay down on the bed. It was too warm for blankets. Above his head, in the coombed ceiling, there was a rooflight. The moon inched its way across the glass. It was so large, so close. He muttered to himself, *My dear friend, my dear friend.*

Eight years later, in 1943, David was amongst a small group of men who met in a house in the Greek village of Petrana. The men with him were members of a resistance group, ELAS, involved in the sabotage of railway bridges. Two of them were drunk and were being roughly disciplined by their leaders, one of whom seemed to have broken a man's jaw. David stood by; he did not like the methods of these people, but they were not under his command. He knew, and disapproved of, their methods. He knew that they shot their German and Italian prisoners, because he had been warned about that by Paddy Leigh Fermor himself, when they had shared a drink in Cairo. But he could not interfere. "You can try to get them to fall into line," Leigh Fermor said, "but ultimately these men will do what they want. They're a pretty tough bunch."

They were due to make contact with another SOE officer, who was arranging the delivery of explosives. The beating of the drunks suddenly stopped, and one of the ELAS men came to tell him of the arrival in the village of the expected officer. He would be brought to the house shortly.

David waited. His mind was on their mission. Timing was important, as the railway line needed to be attacked at five or six points to render it unusable. There would be reprisals— there always were, but the ELAS men knew it. It would be their brothers and cousins who would be arbitrarily rounded up and shot.

He hated the war. He hated the discomfort and the moments of sheer terror that came when you reflected on the fact that if captured you would not be treated as a combatant, even if you were wearing a uniform, as the SOE did. He hated the distrust and the animosities of the Greeks, who disliked each other, it seemed to him, every bit as much as they disliked their occupiers.

He longed to speak English. He longed to have even a few moments with somebody with whom he could share a joke about the flea-ridden beds and the difficulty of shaving and the squabbles of the Greeks.

He asked for something to eat. He had not had a meal for over twenty-four hours, and hunger was gnawing at him. They brought him a bowl of olives, wrinkled and excessively salty, and a chunk of goat's milk cheese, on which mould had grown and had to be dusted off. There was a flask of wine, raw, murky, and dark red. He looked at the wine in his glass and thought of something that had not crossed his mind for a long time. Homer described the sea as being wine-dark. That had lodged in his memory. How could the sea be wine-dark? Did the Ancient Greeks see colour in a different way from the way we saw it? Or did they not care very much and would accept any description that fitted the metre?

It was while he was thinking about this and eating the cheese that into the room, escorted by a tall bearded ELAS man, came Bruce.

For a moment they did not recognise one another, and then they did. David stepped forward first and threw his arms around his friend. He shouted, but did not know what he shouted. He did not care.

"You know one another," said the ELAS man, and smiled.

They sat down. The ELAS people had made coffee. A raid on an Italian transport a few weeks earlier had resulted in distribution of coffee through various networks; some had reached them.

They quickly established where they had been. Neither knew that the other was serving in the same theatre of operations.

"I thought you were in Cairo," said David.

"I was. They recruited me there. SOE."

"Because you'd done some Greek at St. Andrews?"

Bruce smiled. "The Army never fully understood the difference between classical and modern Greek."

They talked about their experiences. "I've been in Macedonia," Bruce said. "Liaison work, for the most part—arranging drops. Arms. Radios. Gold sovereigns to fund the whole thing. And trying to keep the Greeks from killing one another."

David knew of the hatreds, of the plans that the Communists had to take over once the Germans left and the determination of others to thwart them. "What they don't seem to grasp," Bruce went on, "is the fact that once you let the Communist Party in, you'll never get them out. The commissars themselves know that, but the average man doesn't. They see somebody offering them relief from hopeless poverty—and that's enough for them. And who can blame them, when all you have is a herd of goats and a few olive trees?"

"And a procession of priests and stony fields . . ."

Bruce shook his head. "Don't underestimate the priests. I saw one standing in front of a house that the Germans were trying to burn. He was waving an icon at them, but the Germans pushed him out of the way. He got to his feet, but the Germans knocked him down again."

"You were watching?" asked David.

"From a house on the other side of the village square. It was too dangerous to get out at the back. I had to stay and see them set fire to one building after another."

There was more. There was more death. "I've become used to it, you know," said Bruce. "It took me a little time, but you get used to its presence. Death is like the weather. It just happens. And you know something else? I feel I've been doing this forever. I can't imagine what it must be like not to be on the run, hiding, in a different house virtually every night."

"I suppose you do get used to it. I suppose you get used to anything."

"You get used to any sort of life," said Bruce. "You take what's on offer." It was the sort of observation that seemed to be prompted by their circumstances. You talked about life when you knew it could be taken away from you at any moment.

Two hours passed. There was business to be done—explosives had been hidden on a hillside above the village—but they could not move until after dark.

"I don't like this waiting," said Bruce. "I don't mind the actual work—laying the charges, that sort of thing. But this waiting gets to me."

"Of course it does," David agreed. "I close my eyes and try to think of other things. I try to remember the road between Edinburgh and Inverness, imagining every twist and turn. Or I try to remember a novel I've read. I've been remembering some of Scott. That seems to have stuck."

"I never liked Scott," said Bruce. "I could read Stevenson, but not Scott. He takes so long."

David smiled. "They had a lot of time then."

Then Bruce said, "I don't know how to say this."

David looked away. "You don't have to."

"But I think I do. Because it could be tonight, you know. They might be waiting for us. Or tomorrow morning, after the line's gone up. They'll be searching for us. And it could happen very quickly. In a moment or two it could be over—for either of us." He paused. "I wouldn't want it to be you, you know." His voice became a whisper. "I'd cry buckets at your funeral."

David did not say anything.

Then Bruce continued, "I've thought about you just about every day. Every day."

There was silence. Then David said, "I'm glad." He looked down at his hands. The war was on them.

"That's all I wanted to say," said Bruce.

"It's all right," said David.

One of the ELAS men brought them a fresh cup of coffee.

"For your nerves," he said as he gave it to them.

They saw one another in Greece twice after that. David was brought home after being injured in a road accident. It was an ignominious injury, he said: a drunken ELAS driver had gone into a tree when they were on a mission to deliver aid. David was briefly concussed, and during his concussion the gold sovereigns he was carrying as aid to a beleaguered village were stolen from him. Bruce was brought home slightly later. He was awarded the MC for conspicuous bravery. David married two years after the end of the war. His wife was a primary school teacher. They had no children, although there had been a stillbirth. Bruce took over the running of his father's estate, but sold it shortly afterwards. He met an American woman, an artist from Minneapolis, and they married six months later. She liked Scotland and encouraged Bruce to buy a farm near Melrose, in the Borders. They had two daughters, one of whom played hockey for Scotland.

If David and Bruce were asked whether they were happy, both would have replied yes, they were, although there might have been a moment's hesitation before that reply was given. But if you have to hesitate for only a moment in considering that question, then you are probably happy enough, which is as much as most of us can expect.

Their school organised a reunion, at which both Bruce and David were present. The school pipe band played in the quad, although it had started to rain, the soft, intermittent rain of the Scottish Highlands. As he watched the boys marching past in their kilts, the Highland pipes vocal in their lament, David thought: Nobody is going to ask these boys to go to Greece; nobody is going to expect of them what was expected of us. And what was that? To do what needed to be done because a monstrous evil had shown its face? Or because humanity had simply behaved in the way in which it had behaved throughout history, and had squabbled and fought over grubby issues of territory? No, he thought, that is too cynical: it was not like that. It had been far simpler. It had been about bullying and cruelty and the strutting of dark gods.

Bruce stood beside him. David said, "Do you remember something?" Bruce waited. "You said in Greece one day that you'd cry buckets at my funeral. Do you remember?"

Bruce smiled. "Did I say that?"

"Yes. You did."

"Well, I suppose I would."

David felt the rain upon his face. "I meant to say the same thing," he said. He paused. In the lives of most of us, the list of unsaid things was, he thought, a long one.

Sphinx

S HE WAS TWENTY-SIX YEARS OLD, the daughter of a green-grocer from a town on the Firth of Clyde. Her mother had died when she was twelve—a sudden, acute appendicitis—and her father had brought up her and her younger brother with the help of his unmarried sister, a district nurse. Her brother had taken a job in the shipyards when he was sixteen. "He's just a boy," she said. "He's just a wee boy, and there he is with all those men. It's such a pity." Her father had sighed. "Pity or not, he's lucky to have anything these days," he said. It was 1931.

She was called Margaret, which had been her mother's name. Her father said that she had grown into the image of her mother. "She was a fine-looking woman," he said. "Just like you, my darling—just like you."

She blushed at the compliment. There was no vanity in her; she used make-up, but not very much. "Lilies need no gilding," said her aunt. "You have good skin. Good skin is one of the greatest gifts, you know, and you don't need to try to improve it. Remember that."

The aunt knew all about poverty, and its effects on even the strongest and most determined. She had done her training at the Victoria Infirmary, and then been sent to the Gorbals, where she was attached to a partnership of two doctors, both Highlanders who had spent their working lives in the slums of Glasgow. "You get used to the smell of poverty," one of the doctors said to her. "After a while, you don't notice it so much. But it's always there." The aunt listened to this, and told her niece that only hard work stood between her and the world of those Gorbals streets. She was very conscious of status and respectability. "People laugh at these things," she said, "but they wouldn't if they saw what I saw every day of the week."

The advice was heeded. Margaret was diligent at school and found a place at a secretarial college in Glasgow. "That's a good start," said her aunt. "But she could do even better than that. With her brains—and her looks—she could get somewhere."

Her father smiled. "She'll find some nice fellow to marry," he said. "Or he'll find her, rather. Somebody who's made something of himself. Somebody with a good trade—maybe a little business."

"Possibly," said the aunt. "They say good looks marry up, don't they?"

"Perhaps," said her father, and then added, "Except sometimes."

"Don't talk like that," cautioned the aunt.

After Margaret had finished at the secretarial college, she took a job in a bank in Glasgow. She was there for four years, during which she lived as a lodger in a house in the West End. Her aunt approved, as the address was a respectable one. "I think I know the street," she said. "You'll like it there."

The landlady was the widow of a dentist who had drowned on a fishing trip to the Upper Clyde. The dentist's widow was kind to her, and full of advice. She chided Margaret gently for not doing more to find a husband. "The best men are taken early," she said. "Wait too long and you're left with the also-rans." Margaret listened politely, but explained that she had no desire to rush things. "I'll know," she said. "I'll know the right man when he comes along. I'm waiting for him, you see."

"As long as the ship hasn't already sailed," replied the widow. "That's all I'm saying, Margaret."

The manager of the bank, a thin-faced man with a recalcitrant cough, told her one day that he had heard of a vacancy in a London bank. "This is a very good job," he said. "One of their top men—and I mean top—is looking for a replacement for the secretary who's been with him for twenty-seven years. Her eyesight is going and she's retiring. He needs somebody with the right skills. I know him because he's married to my cousin. I could put in a word for you, if you like."

London! But then she wondered where she would live. London was intimidating; you could not just go down to London and find a dentist's widow with a room to let. She was sure it would not be that simple. The manager, though, had anticipated her concern. "My cousin knows a woman from Glasgow. She lives in a place called Notting Hill and takes lodgers. Well-brought-up girls, of course. Two or three of them, I think. My cousin says she could fix you up there."

Her father encouraged her. "It'll be different," he said. "There's a lot to do in London, I'm told. I'm not saying that there's not a lot to do in Glasgow, but London's bigger, you know. More people. More people means more things to do."

"There are many opportunities in London," said her aunt.

"But you have to be careful. The English can be lax, you know."

Margaret took a day or two to decide. Then she told the manager that she would be happy to move; could he have a word with his cousin's husband? "I already have," he said. "The job's yours if you want it."

She went down to London a month later. The room in Notting Hill was light and clean, with curtains made of thick linen. There was a gas fire that was controlled by a coin-fed meter. A hot bath was available on prior notice to the landlady, who had a measuring stick to ascertain the depth of the water with which it was filled. "Some people think you need to wallow," she said. "I don't."

The job in the bank was more demanding than the position she had filled in Glasgow. Her employer spoke quickly when he dictated letters, and he did not like repeating himself. She worked at improving her shorthand, and after a week she was able to keep up with him without too much difficulty. He was courteous, and appreciative of her work. "You Scots know how to work," he said.

"We do our best," said Margaret.

"I can tell that," he replied.

She wondered about his home life. She knew that he was married, and that he lived in a place called Islington. In order to satisfy her curiosity, she had one Saturday taken a bus to his part of town and found the street on which he lived. She knew the number of his house, and walked past it, but on the other side of the road. She looked up as she drew level with the unremarkable terraced house and saw that he was standing in the window, looking down on the street. She immediately averted her eyes, but she was sure that he saw her. Burning with shame, she hurried down the street.

On the following Monday he asked her how she had enjoyed her weekend. She was flustered, and it took her a few moments to reply. Then she said, "I went for a long walk—all around London—places I had never been to before." She paused. "Even your part of town, I think."

He looked at her sideways, obviously uncertain as to how to respond. Then he said, "That's right—I saw you. Or at least I think I saw somebody who looked a lot like you."

She affected surprise. "Really?"

"Yes, I thought you walked by my place—on the other side of the street."

"Possibly. I walked for miles." She made a show of insouciance. "Probably about fifteen miles altogether. I checked up on a map."

He smiled at her. "You don't want to overdo things," he said.

One afternoon, several months later, she was given time off by her boss. He had to go to a meeting in Manchester and the office was quiet. "You can take the afternoon off," he said. "You worked late yesterday and you deserve it."

She left the office shortly after twelve. There was a corner house where she would have lunch—perhaps taking longer over it than she normally would. Then she would go off to Oxford Street to look at the shops. She needed new shoes, and would be able to take her time in finding just the right pair.

The corner house was busy, and she had difficulty finding a table. But then a young man who was already seated indicated that she could take the spare seat opposite him. She thanked him and sat down.

She saw that he was gazing at her.

"I'm called Robert," he said. "Friends call me Bob."

She told him her name.

"I knew a Margaret once," he said. "She sang like a nightingale. She really did. A gorgeous voice."

"I can't sing," said Margaret. "I've tried, but I can't. I think you have to train your vocal cords."

Robert nodded. "Maybe we could go for a walk after lunch," he said. "Down to the river. It's such a fine day."

They walked slowly. Down on the embankment, the sun was on the river, lending it a ripple of gold. Some small boys were throwing stones into the water, shouting out, making the explosive sounds that boys do. A barge was making its stately progress upstream. A ship's horn sounded.

Margaret looked at Robert—a sideways glance. She liked him, and in a sudden moment of insight she said to herself: This is the man. This is the man I've been waiting for. This is the one.

They came to the Needle and the two attendant sphinxes. "I love coming here," he said. "I've always liked the idea of ancient Egypt. Pyramids, sphinxes, what have you. I've always loved that sort of thing."

She gazed up at the sphinx. "You wonder what it's thinking," she said. "It looks as if it knows something, but you can't really tell what it is, can you?"

"That's how they're meant to look," he said. "Enigmatic." He paused. "Yes, I come here just about every week. I look at the hieroglyphs and wonder what they mean."

"Does anybody know?" she asked.

Robert shrugged. "Professors, maybe. They know, I think, but the rest of us just have to guess."

She pointed at the characters. "Maybe that just says: *This way round.*"

He laughed. "That's very funny," he said. "You make me laugh, you know. Oh, in a good way, of course. You're fun."

She blushed.

Then he said, "I have to get back to the office. I'm going to be working late tonight, which is why I've been able to take this time off. But can you give me your address—I'll write to you, if you say you don't mind."

"I don't," she said, hoping that she did not reply too quickly. She gave him the address in Notting Hill. "You have to write *Care of Mrs. Higgs.* She's the landlady, and she's very particular about that sort of thing."

He wrote down the details in a notebook. "Care of Mrs. Higgs," he said. "Good. That's it. I'll send you a postcard and then we can arrange to meet again."

"I'd like that," she said, once again worrying that she might sound too eager. The dentist's widow had advised against that. "Never let them think you're too keen," she said. "Men don't like that. Take my word for it."

She waited anxiously for his postcard. A week passed, and then another one, and her hopes began to fade. After three weeks she decided that he was not going to write. Mrs. Higgs noticed her mood and asked what was wrong. After hearing the story, the landlady said, "I don't think you should write him off. He probably lost his notebook. Men lose things all the time, you know."

That thought preyed on her mind. Eventually she decided that she would go back to the sphinx. He had said that he went there almost every week, and if that were the case she could leave him a message. She would write a note and tuck it between the sphinx's toes. Her message would be that she thought he might have mislaid her address. If he had, then here it was again and she would love to hear from him—only if he wanted to write, of course.

She left the note in the sphinx's toes for three Saturdays in a row, replacing it each week because the paper became damp or washed away. Nothing happened. There was no postcard, no letter. He doesn't want to see me again, she thought. I should take the hint.

She remembered something her aunt had said to her. "Self-pity, if you ask me, is pitiful. If things go wrong, Margaret—and they will, from time to time—don't mope. What you need to do is find something else to think about. I know you young people don't like listening to advice, but that's the truth, you know. Never indulge in self-pity. Never."

What, she wondered, would a person keen to avoid self-pity do in her circumstances? She had been disappointed by a meeting with a man. The answer to that, then, was to set about meeting another man. She would go to a dance. She had seen one advertised—a Saturday-afternoon dance in a hall not far from where she lived. Refreshments would be served, she read, and music would be by a "rising band, talked about across half London." She wondered who talked about bands, and why only half London was talking about this one. Why only half London? What about the other half?

She bought a new dress for the occasion and was one of the first people admitted to the dance hall. "You're keen," said a woman in the ladies'. "Like me. The early bird catches the worm, they say, don't they?"

She laughed nervously. "I don't really know. It's my first time here."

The woman smiled. "Don't worry, dear. You'll have no trouble. They'll all want to dance with you—it's when you get to my age that the field thins out a bit."

"Are there . . ." She was not sure how to say it. Surely you shouldn't talk about men as if they were cattle at a cattle market. But how else could you put it? "Are there plenty of *spare* fellows?"

The woman clearly found this amusing. "Plenty of spare fellows? Oh, my goodness, all of them are spare. That's why they come here. It's how they find a girl. That's the way it works, you know." She paused. "This isn't a church social, you know."

She did not know how to respond. But her new friend continued, "Mind you, they're not a bad lot, the men who come here. It's because you get a good class of man coming here that I choose to patronise the place myself. Men with decent jobs. Respectable men. Men whose fingernails are at least clean." There was another pause. "Oh, I can tell you about some places where you can't count on that. You get rough men, you see—the types who have grime under their fingernails. I can't stand that, you know. Gives me the shudders."

Margaret said, "I don't think I'd like that."

"No. Who would? Anyway, you come in with me and we'll find a place to sit and listen to the band. The fellows will arrive sure enough—give them time."

They went into the hall. The hall's lighting was subdued, and the dance floor itself was a pool of darkness in the centre of the room. The band, seated on a dais at the far end of the hall, consisted of half a dozen musicians. A clarinet player, standing up for his solo, was delivering a popular melody. She recognised it, and thought of the words. It was all about heart-strings and how they could be tugged when you were least expecting it. Perhaps it would happen to her today, just as the song said it could. Songs, of course, did not always get it right, but they must be right at least sometimes. People did meet people who inspire them and whom they want to meet again. She had already done that, although she told herself that she should not think about him—that she should not think about sphinxes—especially not when she was trying to meet somebody else.

Her friend was talking about a film she had seen. Margaret was not paying close attention to what was being said, and her mind had drifted when the man came over to speak to her.

"He's asking you, dear," whispered the woman.

She stood up, taking the man's hand as she did so. She let

him lead her onto the dance floor, where already a few couples were circling.

He introduced himself. "My name's Alfred, by the way."

She gave him her name.

"You don't like to be called Peggy?"

She shook her head. She had never encouraged that. "And you? Do you like people to call you Alf?"

He looked disapproving. "I think you should stick to the name your parents give you. I feel that quite strongly."

As they started to dance, she looked at him surreptitiously. He wasn't bad-looking, she thought. In fact, when he turned his head to the side, he was more than that—quite good-looking, she decided. And he was about the right age too—a bit older than she was, she imagined, but not yet thirty. It was too early, she told herself, to be going out with a man of thirty.

They danced in silence. When the band came to the end of the tune, he thanked her formally and asked her whether she would like some tea and cake. "They have a very nice sponge cake here, you know. Very fine."

She wondered how he knew. He must come here regularly to have formed a view on the cake they served.

"I'd love a cup of tea," she said. "Dancing makes you thirsty, I think."

He considered this, seeming to weigh the observation as if it were of some profundity. At length he delivered his verdict. "Some dancing does that," he said. "On the other hand, you can feel quite hot just sitting down. It's the lights, I think. They generate heat."

She looked up at the lights. They were bright, at least round the edge of the room, but she could not think of anything much to say about them.

"We had a power cut the other day," Alfred suddenly remarked. "We were sitting in the front room listening to the Light Programme on the wireless, and suddenly everything went dark."

"You must have been worried," she said.

He considered this too. "Maybe. A bit. But then, when the lights go out suddenly like that, you realise that it's probably a power cut. That's what I thought, anyway."

"Oh."

"Yes. And my mother was in the room too. She was listening to the wireless with me, and of course the BBC went off the air. Just silence."

"I suppose, with the power going off . . ."

"Yes," he agreed. "The wireless couldn't work without electricity. But then, you know what my mother said? She said: You'd think the lights wouldn't go off while you're listening to the Light Programme. The Light Programme, you see—a different sort of light, of course."

She laughed dutifully, but she found herself looking towards the door. It was too early to make an excuse, but she would do so, in twenty minutes, perhaps—after they had drunk their tea and eaten the sponge cake. Twenty minutes could be endured.

He went to fetch the tea. While he was away, she saw the woman she had met in the ladies'. She was on the dance floor now, in the arms of a tall man with slicked-back hair and protruding teeth. She caught Margaret's eye and waved; Margaret thought she winked, but could not be sure.

Alfred put the cup of tea in front of her.

"Don't let it get cold," he warned. "There's nothing worse than cold tea."

She wanted to say, "Oh, but there are plenty of things far worse." But she simply smiled and raised the cup to her lips.

"If you're wondering what I do," he said, "I'm a road engineer. I work in the office most of the time—deciding which roads we'll repair next. You won't find me out on the streets—looking into a ditch or anything like that."

She realised that this was a joke, and she laughed. "You don't operate one of those signs that says *Go,* do you?"

"Oh, heavens no. We have Irishmen to do that. That's Paddy's job."

"Are they all Irish?" she asked.

"Oh yes. Most of them. Nice fellows, for the most part. Except when they get involved in a fight. You have to be careful then. They take their fights seriously. And horses too. They love their horses, the Irish."

"I suppose they're just people, like the rest of us."

He frowned. "To a certain extent," he said.

Suddenly she asked him, "Would you ever like to visit the pyramids?"

He looked puzzled. "No, not really. It's very hot out there."

"In Egypt?"

"Yes. They're on the edge of the desert, aren't they? I don't like the thought of that. Or the flies. Egypt has lots of flies, I'm told. The pyramids are probably crawling with them."

She looked at her watch. And then, impulsively, she blurted out, "Oh no! I've forgotten. It's Mrs. Higgs's birthday and I was going to get her flowers."

He asked who Mrs. Higgs was.

"My landlady. She's been very good to me. Her daughter told me that today was her birthday, and I wanted to surprise her." She looked at her watch again. "I hope you don't mind. I really need to go."

He shook his head. "I don't mind at all," he said. "In fact, I'm not all that keen on the band. I'll come and help you get the flowers. Do you mind?"

She hesitated, and then replied, "No. That's kind of you."

They bought the flowers—a large bunch of red and white carnations. He said, "I'll see you home safely," as they left the florist.

"It's really not necessary." She was wondering what she would do with the flowers. The birthday was a lie—a pretext— and she was not sure where she would find a vase for the flowers. Perhaps she could give them to Mrs. Higgs anyway, as a general thank-you present for being a thoughtful landlady.

"I'd like to," he said. "You shouldn't wander about London too much on your own. Not these days."

"It's not all that late."

He brushed aside her objections. "There are always undesirables. Always."

She wondered whether, being a road engineer, he was privy to information she did not have; perhaps road engineers knew where the undesirables were.

She was firm at the door of the house. "I must say good-night here," she said. "Mrs. Higgs doesn't permit visitors."

"No," he said. "Very wise."

"So, goodnight, Alfred. And thank you . . . for the tea and cake."

"It was my pleasure."

She waited for him to go.

"Would you come to tea with me and my mother?" he asked. "She'd love to meet you. I know she would." He paused. "She has albums of photographs of her trips to France. She's been five times. She speaks a bit of French, you see."

She closed her eyes. She should say no; she should make it clear. But instead she said, "That would be very kind."

"Next Saturday?"

She suppressed a sigh. "Yes. Next Saturday."

His mother was called Annette. She wore her hair in a bun.

"I don't speak a lot of French," she said. "I learned it at school, of course, as we all did, but school French is so different, isn't it? All this business about *la plume de ma tante*. Whoever imagined that an aunt's pen might be found in the *garden*?"

Margaret shook her head. "I have no idea."

"No, nor do I. I found, though, that if I talked to people—actually talked to them—I learned a lot. And the French don't mind talking French, you know—in fact, they like to talk French, I find."

The conversation continued. The photograph albums were

produced and discussed. Alfred said very little, and when he went out of the room to put the kettle back on, Annette leaned towards Margaret and whispered, "He's a lovely boy, you know. He lacks confidence—that's all."

She did not know what to say.

Then Annette continued, "Don't rush him. Let him take things at his own speed."

She opened her mouth to speak. But Annette kept going, "He'll treat you well, my dear. His father was a real gentleman. He was an engineer too—a different sort, though. He was mainly bridges. Alfred picked things up from him. That's where the engineering came from. There's always an explanation for everything. We don't become what we become by accident."

Margaret asked how her interest in France had arisen.

Annette thought for a moment. "I heard somebody speaking French," she said. "And I thought: I'd like to be able to do that. That's how it happened, I think. Amazing."

Three months later, Alfred said to her, "How long have we been seeing one another?"

She shrugged. "A few months."

"Yes," he said. "A few months."

She waited. She had decided that she would have to tell him. It was unfair of her to continue to let him think that this would develop into something. She had accepted his invitations only because she had had nothing else to do and she felt sorry for him. He was lonely—and she was lonely too; there was no harm in going to the dance hall together or to the cinema. And in the cinema it was hard to push him away from her, and she had succumbed to the hand-holding that he seemed to like. They held hands throughout the film, and it made their palms hot and sticky—not that he seemed to mind.

And now here he was about to say something that would put her in a spot. She would have to speak.

"I think I'm going to go back to Glasgow," she said, adding, "next week."

He stared at her in dismay. "Glasgow?" he stuttered.

She nodded. "My aunt is unwell. She needs me to look after her."

It was pure invention, and she felt a momentary pang: You should not lie about people's health, she thought. You bring about the thing you invent. That was the danger.

He seemed reassured. "Oh, just until she's better . . ."

"Which won't be for a long time," she said. "My aunt's very ill."

"I'm sorry. What is it? Do you mind my asking?"

She looked at the floor. "I'd prefer not to talk about it."

"It isn't polio, is it?"

She shook her head. "It's her chest."

"TB?"

"I said, I'd prefer not to talk about it." She closed her eyes. "Her heart, actually. Her heart is enlarged."

"Oh . . ."

"Yes. It's all swollen up."

"I'm sorry."

"So I have to go, Alfred."

He looked anguished. "As it happened, I was going to say . . ."

"No," she said. "It's best not to talk about it."

That would have been her opportunity to end it, but the following day she sent him a postcard to tell him that her aunt had made a dramatic recovery. She had felt guilty over the lie. She thought: You have to take the person you are allocated in this life. She had been given Alfred, and she should accept it. There were plenty of much duller men in London—she had met a number of them—and he would be solid and reliable. She could do far worse.

He told her how delighted he was that she would not be returning to Glasgow. "I'd like to take you out to dinner," he said. "Not just an ordinary meal. I'd like to go somewhere special. We could make it a special occasion."

She knew immediately what he meant, and that this, rather than the dinner itself, was the moment of decision. He would ask her to marry him. She had allowed this situation to develop. She had drifted into something, in the way in which we are all capable of drifting into things, without any conscious assertion of will, any firm choice, because it is easy and we feel sorry for people and we cannot find a simple way of avoiding their emotional claims. She should have found an excuse not to go out to dinner, but she did not, because her drift had continued, and now it was too late.

I have one last afternoon, she thought. I have one last afternoon as myself before I become an engaged woman. She went for a walk, almost in a daze, conscious that her future was approaching her like a car on a dark road, and she was caught in its headlights. She walked through Bedford Square. She stopped to talk to a woman selling flowers, who gave her some sort of blessing she could not understand, but in which the words *good luck* stood out. She stopped to help a child who had tripped and grazed his knees. She gave him her handkerchief to wipe away the tiny lines of blood. He looked up at her and smiled, and she used the handkerchief to attend to his streaming nose. And then, a short distance away, behind the glass of a noticeboard, she saw the announcement of an exhibition of Egyptian artefacts. This was in the British Museum, and it was free. She hesitated, and then went in. He loved ancient Egypt—he had told her that.

She saw him standing next to a roll of papyrus. An ancient clerk had covered the papyrus with hieroglyphs. Her heart beating loudly within her, she approached him.

He turned and saw her. She had half-expected his face to fall, as it can do when we encounter somebody we hoped to avoid. But this did not happen. He smiled broadly and reached out for her hand. He said he could not believe it. He had been distraught at the loss of the notebook in which he had noted her address. How does one find a lost person in London? It was impossible.

"Have you been down to the Sphinx?" she asked.

He looked puzzled. "No, I've been a bit busy."

He pointed to the papyrus. "Look at that," he said. "Think how old that is."

She stared at the faint text.

"What does it say?" she asked.

He looked down. "It says: *I love you very much.*"

"Really?"

"Yes, and then it says, *I am glad we have found one another.*"

She bent down to examine the symbols more closely. Somebody had written these all those years ago; somebody had actually touched this paper all those years ago.

"Does it really say that?" she asked. "Does it really?"

He smiled. "No," he said. "That's me talking."

Maternal Designs

H E IS AN ARCHITECT, this man in the white shirt and the dark suit, striding away purposefully from the half-collapsed building in the background. The dust made him sneeze; it always did, and the only thing to do was get away from it as soon as possible. He has seen enough, anyway, and now he is making his way back home, to talk to his mother. She will be sitting in the living room when he gets back—the tea things laid out on the table—sitting there as if butter wouldn't melt in her mouth, he thought.

His name was Richard, and he had been in practice as an architect for nine years. He had been born into construction, as he liked to put it, his father having been a successful builder in Stirling. His mother, the daughter of a Dundee jute merchant, had been ambitious for her son, and had discouraged talk of his following his father into the business.

"You could go to university," she said to him shortly before his sixteenth birthday. "You've got a good brain, Dickie, and you're a hard worker. You could even go to somewhere down south. Maybe even Cambridge." She waved a hand in the direction of England. In fact, it was Bannockburn, which lay not too far away from where they lived. A previous owner, strangely, had named their house "Battle View"; she would have changed it, as she thought it in bad taste, but had heard somewhere that it was bad luck to change a house's name. A neighbour in Broughty Ferry had done that, and had died the next day. That was pure coincidence—obviously—but why tempt providence?

He expressed doubt. Cambridge seemed very unlikely, and he was not sure that he would like the people down there. They seemed to consider themselves superior in some way, and he had never approved of that sort of thing. Quite apart from that, though, he did not think of himself as a high-flier. "I'm not that clever, Ma. There are plenty of fellows who get better marks than I do."

She would not have him selling himself short. "Nonsense. Who got the Rector's prize for effort last year? You did. That counts for something."

"But there are plenty of places I could go in Scotland. Or I could work with Daddy in the firm. He said I could, you know. He said he'd like that."

She shook her head. "Boys who work with their fathers end up fighting with them. It often happens that way. Time and time again. That Henderson boy, for example. He and his father didn't talk for years. And then what happened? Bobby Henderson dropped dead on the golf course and that boy didn't have the chance to make his peace with him. I don't want the two of you falling out."

"But what if I want . . ."

She did not let him finish. "I'm not saying there's anything wrong with being a builder, Dickie. If you think I'm saying that, you're wrong."

He thought: Don't call me Dickie! Don't call me Dickie! I'm not a little boy any more.

"No, there's nothing wrong with being a builder. Your daddy's done really well—as you know. All those houses for people to live in. Decent houses too. With hot water and so on. With good windows for fresh air—and light too. Light's very important, you know. Consumption flourishes where there's no light."

"How? What has light to do with it?"

"Germs don't like sunlight. They can't thrive in sunlight. You saw that photograph in that magazine—remember?"

He did remember. There had been a photograph in his mother's magazine of a group of children lying on reclining chairs in the Swiss mountains. It was a sanatorium, his mother explained, and the children in the photographs were all consumptive. "Poor dears," she said. "Not their fault."

They were bare-chested, even the young girls, but he paid attention only to their sunglasses.

"Why are they all wearing dark glasses?"

"Because of the sun. It's very bright up in the Swiss mountains. You need sunglasses to protect your eyes."

He studied the photograph. "Will they all die?" he asked his mother.

She hesitated. "No, I'm sure they're already getting better. See—they look as if they've been putting on weight. No ribs to be seen."

But their ribs *did* show, he thought; and they would all be dead by now. She was trying to protect him.

"The point is," she said, "I happen to think that it's best for a boy not to work with his father. It just leads to difficulties."

She looked pensive. "I think that medicine would be a good career for you, you know. You could become a surgeon, perhaps. You'd like that."

He met her stare. *She* would like that—that's what she meant. *She* would like it.

"I don't like the sight of blood," he said. "It makes me . . . it makes me shiver. I go all cold."

She laughed this off. "Nonsense. You don't feel cold. That's your imagination at work. And remember, you're sixteen now. You might have felt that when you were younger—nine or ten, perhaps—but you're much older now."

"I should know how I feel."

She shot him a discouraging glance. "We all change. All of us. I remember I used to hate mustard. And now? I love it. You can't go through life saying *I hate mustard* because that is shutting off the possibility of change. We all change. All the time—as we go through life, we change."

He looked away. He wanted to lead his own life. He wanted it to be on his terms.

"I suppose if you don't like medicine, you could be a chemist. That's an interesting job. Chemists have an interesting time—mixing medicines and so on. There's a lot to being a chemist these days."

"I don't want that. I don't like the smell of their shops. It's something to do with disinfectant, or something. I don't like it. It makes me sneeze."

"Nonsense," she said. "And try to be a bit more positive, darling. You have to do something—you can't just wait for the world to choose something for you to do."

But he had chosen. He wanted to build things. It was a desire that lay deep within him. He wanted to build, and he told her so, again.

She nodded. She did not want him to think that she was not prepared to listen to him; she was. But listening was not the same thing as agreeing.

"It's always better if a son goes off and does something different. And university broadens the mind. Everybody knows that, Dickie."

"But, as I've said, I like building things," he protested.

"I know that, darling. But there's more to life than that. You want to be an educated man, don't you? Of course you do. You want to be able to look anybody in the eye, anybody, and say—to yourself, naturally, not out loud—*I'm every bit as good as he is.*"

He did not argue, and when he was seventeen he applied to the College of Art in Edinburgh for admission to the course in architecture. His mother accepted the situation, even though she continued to hope he would change his mind and opt for medicine. "Still," she said, "architecture is a solid profession. There are some very well-known architects in Edinburgh. They get a lot of attention." She paused. "Mind you, I can't see why they need all that training. Designing a building is mostly common sense, I would have thought."

"It's not that simple, Ma," he said. "You have to know about stresses and strains."

She shrugged. "Make the walls thick enough. Use strong timbers. They never used to have architects, you know. They got by."

He thought, You don't know what you're talking about, Ma. Sorry, but you don't.

After graduation he took a job with a firm of architects called Gordon, Patrick and Gordon. One of the Gordons was the president of a golf club. "I want to talk to you about golf," he said, shortly after Richard had joined the firm. "Could we have lunch together—at my golf club? Any day that suits you."

Richard had not known what to expect. At first the conversation had been about the office, and about the firm's plans to expand. But then, after a slightly awkward silence, Mr. Gordon had said, "I know that some people have very little time for golf. I can't understand that myself, but there we are."

"It seems to me to be a reasonably enjoyable game," said Richard. "And it keeps you fit, I imagine."

"Oh, it does that, all right," said Mr. Gordon. "But it does much more than that. It brings in business—a lot of business." He paused and gave Richard an intense look. "That's why I've one piece of advice for you, Richard: Play golf. That's all I have to say on the matter."

"I see," said Richard.

He did not take up golf, and nothing more was said of the matter as he progressed up the rungs of his profession. After a mere five years, he had under his control some of the most important and lucrative contracts in the firm's portfolio. His mother was inordinately proud of him. "Dickie is one of the most talented architects of our day," she boasted to her friends. "And, do you know, he lets me look at his designs before they go off to the client. He values my views, you know, and if I think that something's not right, he usually pays very close attention to what I have to say.

"The problem, you see," Richard's mother continued, "is that many architects simply forget to ask women what they want. If you're designing a house for a couple, any couple, an architect should bear in mind what women need—and want. Men are indifferent to heating—women are not. And men don't care about floor surfaces. They don't. And because architects are almost always men, they don't know what women's requirements are."

"Women should tell them," said Richard. "They should spell it out to men what they need in a house."

His mother smiled grimly. "One day women will find their rightful place. Men will have to stop thwarting us."

He tried to persuade her that men were not thwarting women, but he did not succeed. "Look at me," she retorted. "I would have made a very good architect. Yes, I know I'm saying that myself, but I know I would. But it's very difficult. There was just a handful—a mere handful, Dickie—of women architects until a few years ago, you know. Hardly any. Men kept us out."

His eyes widened. "I'm sorry."

"Yes, well, there you are. Men kept women out of everything. They still do."

He looked down at his feet. He did not argue. All you had to do, he thought, was think about it from the women's point of view, and the injustices became apparent. That was the trick, he told himself. Put yourself in the other's shoes and the world looked very different.

After his father died, the building company was sold. Richard had decided that he needed a change of surroundings and had taken a job in a larger firm in London. With the legacy he received from his father's estate, he bought a flat in Earl's Court, in a slightly run-down mansion block overlooking a leafy square. After he had been there for three months, his mother told him that she, too, had decided to move to London. She told him this when he was back in Scotland for the wedding of a school friend.

"I need to stretch my wings," she said. "I find Stirling so . . . so sleepy."

He received the news in silence.

"Well, aren't you pleased?" she asked.

"Very," he said. He made an effort, and said, "Yes, it's very good news. Think of all the things you can do."

"I'm glad you see it that way," she continued. "And you're right—there'll be any number of things for me to do. I shall be positively exhausted."

He smiled. "Don't overdo it, of course."

"I shan't. There'll be bridge, naturally. I've heard of a club near Berkeley Square that's looking for members. Fosty Anstruther belongs. She said you need to be introduced, and she'll do that for me. And she's told me about a course she goes on for people interested in architectural history."

This was a novelty. "Architectural history?"

"Yes, buildings. Movements in architecture—that sort of

thing. Fosty says that they're going to Rome on a field trip next year. Imagine that. Rome! I shall probably see Mussolini himself."

"Thug. Bully."

"So they say. But he's frightfully interested in architecture himself, Fosty says."

He reflected on this in silence. Then he asked, "Where are you going to live?"

"Well, I was going to ask you about that. Do you think you might be able . . . to put me up for a while?" She laughed. "In your bachelor establishment?"

He stared out of the window. The oak tree in the garden moved its boughs in the wind.

"Dickie?"

"Yes. I'm thinking."

"I wouldn't get in your way. And I could look for somewhere while I'm staying with you."

He swallowed. "Of course, Ma. You can stay as long as you like."

"You're really kind, Dickie."

"Anything for you, Ma."

He looked out of the window again. You couldn't refuse your own mother, even if sometimes you thought . . . Well, what did you think? You thought that it would be better if she could just give you some room to be yourself.

She did not stay long. After six weeks, her friend, Fosty Anstruther, found a mews house to lease in Chelsea. It had a small garden and a sitting room decorated in the Arts and

Crafts style. Fosty's own lease had come to an end, and she suggested that it might suit both of them if they shared the house. There was more than enough room for the two of them, and it would be an economy too.

Richard thought it a very good idea. "Fosty's good company for you, Ma. I would have worried about you if you were living alone. Of course, I could always keep an eye on you . . ."

She laughed. "Like the little boy in that poem by A. A. Milne? What was his name? James James Morrison Morrison—something like that. He took such care of his mother although he was only three."

"Of course his mother went off by herself," said Richard. "And look what happened to her."

"I suspect she had a good time," she retorted. "Not that Mr. Milne will tell us exactly what she got up to."

Richard met a young woman called Alice Meadows, and they married a year later. She had been a nurse and had spent three years nursing sailors in Portsmouth. He doted on her, and she on him.

"My husband," she said to a friend, "is the perfect husband. He really is. I could try to think of a flaw—and, heaven knows, most men have them in spades—but, honestly, I can't. I just can't."

They hoped for children, but none arrived. "Maybe one day," she said. "Who knows?"

"It doesn't matter," he said. "We have each other. That's the important thing. And I'm happy." He paused. "Are you?"

"Am I happy? Of course I am. I have everything."

He looked at her fondly. "I'm the luckiest man in London."

"And I'm the luckiest woman. By far."

But there was something that had been preying on his mind. Fosty's son, Keith, had moved to Australia and had invited his mother to visit him in Sydney for six months. Richard was concerned about his mother being all by herself, and he discussed with Alice the possibility that she might move in with them for the duration of Fosty's absence. Alice was generous, and needed no persuading. "Of course she can come and live with us. We've got the room. We can turn that storeroom at the back into a sitting room for her, so that she has her own place, more or less. You're the architect, Richard—can you do that?"

"Easily. I'll get somebody to make some shelves. A new carpet will brighten the place up."

Once his mother moved in, she settled quickly, and they were soon all used to the situation.

"Are you happy, Ma?" he asked one day.

"Yes," she replied. "I'm happy. I miss Daddy, of course, but who wouldn't, after all those years of marriage? And I miss Fosty too, I suppose. Although she'll be back before too long. She says she finds Australia very dry."

"But you have enough to do? Enough to keep yourself occupied?"

"I think so. I have my bridge afternoons and—" She broke off.

He did not realise what it was that she did not mention— that discovery was to come later, at a cocktail party in a house in a neighbouring square. The hostess, who was called Maud Prior, known as the Priory, was the daughter of one of his mother's bridge friends, a woman she had occasionally mentioned.

"Your mother and mine get on famously," said the Priory. "Not only do they play bridge together, but they've taken to going to the theatre. A whole group of them went off to see that Coward play the other day. The one about hay fever."

"They keep themselves busy," said Richard.

"And she did a lovely job on that new scullery for my mother's house in Suffolk."

Richard frowned. "Who did?"

"Your mother."

He looked puzzled. "My mother did what?"

The Priory spoke in a rather reedy, High Church voice. "She drew the plans for the new maternal scullery, darling. One's mother does *need* a scullery, you know . . ."

He stared in incomprehension. "You're saying that my mother—*my* mother—designed *your* mother's new scullery?"

The Priory nodded before continuing, "And Mummy's friend Tatania Potts . . . She has a conservatory, you know—designed by your mother. She was very imaginative with that one, I'm told. They had a few teething problems, I gather, but everything's settled down now. They're frightfully pleased with it, although Tatania's husband is a terrible old bore, you know, and drinks far too much."

He was at a loss for words. The Priory looked at him and smiled. "Fosty acted as a sort of assistant, I think. Sharpened the pencils, drew some of the plans—under supervision, of course. Fosty always fancied herself as an artist. Personally, I think her work is a bit . . . how shall I put it, a bit *juvenile*. She thinks she's Augustus John, but . . . Well, the important thing is that your mother is doing rather well in her little architectural practice. So nice. Having a mother who does *nothing* must be very trying. Mine just causes trouble, and that, I suppose, is better than nothing, but sometimes I wish she would get it into her head to do something other than play bridge and gossip . . ."

He raised it with her that evening. "Ma," he said, trying to sound as severe as possible, "you shouldn't be doing this. Architecture is a specialised business. You can't just draw any old thing and get people to build it."

"All right, dear. I won't. I won't practise architecture."

But he suspected that she had no intention of doing as he had asked, and now, with this disaster—this utter disaster—of the part-collapse of the new insurance building he had designed, he knew that his suspicions had been well founded.

He confronted her when he returned from the site. "Ma," he said, his voice rising in anger, "I am really, really cross. Did you fiddle about with those plans I left in my study? Did you touch them?"

She affected a look of innocence. "Me? Your study?"

"Yes," he said, fixing her with an unrelenting stare.

She turned away. "Maybe a little," she muttered. "The offices at the front were too small. I rubbed out a wall—just a small one, though. It gave them much more room."

He closed his eyes. Then he opened them. "Ma," he said, his voice choked. "You must promise me: Never, never do that again."

"Of course, dear," she said. "Of course."

He looked at her, and she looked back at him. "I have to go to bridge now," she said. And then she added, "And Fosty comes back from Australia next week. I'm excited, Dickie—so excited. We have *so many* plans, and my head"—she tapped her forehead lightly—"is positively abuzz."

The Dwarf Tale-Teller
of the Romanian Rom

D R. EDWINA MACLEOD was an anthropologist who had worked with Margaret Mead in Samoa. Mead, whose great work, *Coming of Age in Samoa,* first published in 1928 and regarded as one of the classics of cultural anthropology, enjoyed a considerable reputation as an interpreter of the mores of South Sea adolescents. Edwina was only an occasional collaborator, and features in none of the papers that Mead published, nor in any of her letters to the learned societies that supported her work. Mead had a stamp bearing her image and a high school named after her; Edwina attracted none of these accolades, spending her entire academic career in two low-ranking colleges in upstate New York. Her relative obscurity, though, meant that she avoided the criticism directed against her more illustrious colleague. According to a number of later detractors, Mead's conclusions as to what Samoan teenage girls got up to was based on the testimony of a handful of unreliable informants, one of whom eventually admitted that they were feeding the anthropologist lurid stories as a joke. Anthropologists, it was suggested, are obvious targets of those who enjoy hoaxing others with fanciful stories. If life is dull—as it often is for teenagers—then the presence of a cultural anthropologist might be just too much of a temptation.

Edwina's first opportunity to do work in the field came in 1927, when she responded to an advertisement placed in

The Proceedings of the Anthropological Society of Washington.
This revealed that the society had an unexpended portion
of a grant that had been allocated for research in South-East
Asian anthropology. The grant in question had been taken
up by one Professor George Hopkinson, who for some years
had been researching into the social context of the outlawed,
but then still surviving, practice of headhunting amongst the
Buyaya people. Hopkinson had published several papers on
ritual violence and the incorporation of otherness, based on
his three years in the field. The grant was intended to run for a
total of five years, and so two years' worth remained unspent.
This was a result of Professor Hopkinson's failure to return
from the field. Attempts had been made to contact him, to
no avail, and the conclusion was reached that he had aban-
doned anthropology for some other pursuit. A puzzling note
had been received by the local authorities in Luzon, written
in Melanesian pidgin, and on a scrap of much-handled paper.
This read: *Hopkinson bilong America bilong anthropology he go
long time bilong navy good bye.* Nobody was sure what weight,
if any, should be given to this message, although it seemed to
confirm that Professor Hopkinson would not be returning.
In the circumstances the society decided to make the remain-
ing grant available to a scholar who would continue with the
promising research that he had begun but left unfinished. It
was into this breach that Edwina stepped, in spite of the anxiety that a number of her friends expressed about the project.

"Why study headhunting?" asked one. "Surely it's the sort
of thing one should just leave well alone."

"And what's there to study?" asked another. "One group goes off and chops off the head of a member of another group. So, what's there to say about that?"

She smiled patiently. "There's more to headhunting than you might imagine," she explained. "Headhunting is about defining community. In taking the head of an outsider and bringing it back to the village shrine, the boundaries of the domestic—the local—are clarified. The victim comes from *beyond*. In bringing him—or his head—into the fold, the community is entrenched as an actor. This is a collaborative venture in which the victim himself collaborates—although somewhat unwillingly. The *we* of the venture is set against the *them*. That's an important element in the headhunting rituals and songs in which the village re-creates its history."

"So they sing about it too?" asked an incredulous friend.

Edwina nodded. "Yes," she said.

Her research in the field went well, although the village to which she attached herself appeared to be more interested in weaving than headhunting. She did, however, transcribe a number of songs in which headhunting raids were commemorated, and these were duly published in the society's *Proceedings,* along with a translation and commentary. Shortly before her return to the United States, a woman in the village, one of the weavers with whom Edwina had become friendly, took her in secret to a shrine in the jungle and showed her the village treasures. These included what might have been several human heads, wrapped in reeds and placed on a candelabra-type wooden stand. Pointing to one of these, the woman uttered the word *Hopk,* a term she was unable to translate and which remains something of a mystery.

On her return to the United States, Edwina attended a number of anthropological conferences at which she gave well-received papers based on her field-work. It was at one of these conferences that she met another anthropologist, James Bunker Hall. He was dean of undergraduate studies at a liberal arts college in Ohio, and was the author of a major study of consanguinity in Appalachia. James was a friend of Edward Hopper, the artist, and displayed two of his early watercolours on the wall of his decanal office. It was through James that Edwina met the Hoppers and formed a firm friendship. The two couples occasionally toured New England together, and in the summer, when colleges were on vacation, would spend weekends on Cape Cod, walking on beaches and looking up at the cloud-swept skies that Hopper would later faithfully record in his painting.

Edwina expected James to propose to her, and on several occasions she imagined that he came close to doing this. But he never did so, and in mid-July one summer he announced that he had been offered, and had accepted, a dean's job at Tulane University in New Orleans.

"I'll look into something for you down there," he said to Edwina. "There may be something at Baton Rouge, perhaps. Or Tulane. I'll do what I can."

At first, he wrote regularly, every other week, but gradually his letters became less frequent—and less informative. Eventually they were replaced by the occasional postcard, on which a terse message might be scribbled. *So busy. Students*

want this, that, and the next thing. Never satisfied. One fresh-
man in trouble with the cops. Another had all his clothing stolen
in the French Quarter. All of it! Will write again soon, Bunk.

But he did not. She thought of him often, and then less frequently. From time to time she would utter his name *sotto voce,* as the superstitious might intone a magic word. She blushed when she found herself doing that, and tried to put him out of her mind. Eventually he became no more than a slightly fuzzy memory—as a memory of happiness or contentment might be. She did not regret him, and she felt no anger or resentment. Love does not keep a tally, she reminded herself. Love does not count the replies it receives, or does not receive, to its letters or its postcards.

Edwina is the woman seated in the foreground of the photograph, next to the other woman in the picture, who is wearing a shawl and waiting, against the advice of the popular adage, for a kettle to boil. The kettle, partly obscured by the smoke of the fire, is suspended from a curved iron spit, but seems far too high above the half-hearted flames below. Such a kettle might take a considerable time to come to a boil, one might imagine—perhaps a whole day, or even a day and a half. The disconsolate look of those ranged around the camp-fire certainly points in this direction—these are not people who are anticipating the serving of coffee within the next few minutes.

Although Edwina was at the time an associate professor at a college near Buffalo, this particular photograph clearly portrays field-work being carried out far away from that well-tended campus. Supporting documentary evidence points to its having been taken in 1936, in Romania, where Edwina spent more than a year on a project supported by a generous grant from one of her college's benefactors. Part of this time was spent in Bucharest, but periods of up to a week at a time were spent in the field, not just in the metaphorical sense. In this photograph she is, indeed, in a field—probably one in the foothills of the Transylvanian mountains. Bucharest would have been a long day's train journey away, and the pleasures of its café society might well have been on the anthropologist's mind as she sat waiting for the weak cup of acorn coffee that would in due course be offered.

Edwina's decision to undertake field-work in Romania followed upon a conversation she had in 1934 with a member of the council of the American Society of Social Anthropology, which held its annual conference that year in Boston. The council member was a noted professor at Harvard and the author of an important work on the life of Irish travellers, then known, as they still are in some quarters, as gypsies. This book had introduced readers to the lore and language of those whom many regarded with disdain. It showed that such groups had a culture and institutions that were complex and often misunderstood by a predominantly hostile majority community. In particular, it recorded the rich and vivid stories that Irish gypsies told one another around their firesides. These stories—peopled by all sorts of leprechauns, water spirits, and fairies of every description—were later to be more widely popularised by folklorists, but were well received by those who read this Harvard anthropologist's pioneering work.

"You should look at some of these gypsy communities," the professor advised Edwina. "I'm sure that Margaret (Mead) would agree with me."

Edwina expressed an interest, and this led to a more specific suggestion from the professor.

"Of course, you should go to the heart of the culture," he said. "Go to the source, which is Romania. That's where the real material is to be found."

Edwina wondered what aspect of gypsy life she should study, and this led to the response, "Well, there's something I would look at if I were a bit younger . . ."

And if you didn't have your very comfortable chair at Harvard College, thought Edwina.

". . . yes, if I were a bit younger, I'd go off and look at the dwarf tale-tellers of the Romanian Rom."

Edwina was intrigued, and asked for more details.

"The dwarf tale-tellers," the professor explained, "are a little-known phenomenon outside the world of Transylvanian gypsiology. Professor von Kruse, you may have met—no, perhaps not: I don't think he was ever up in Buffalo—anyway, von Kruse did some work on them back in the early twenties."

Edwina so resented the assumptions in this conversation. She accepted that her college was not in the same league as Harvard—nowhere near it, in fact—but she and her colleagues had their contribution to make and could do without the condescension of Ivy Leaguers. But these were thoughts you did not express, because everybody knew where academic patronage and power lay, and it was not in obscure colleges in upstate New York, nor anywhere similar, for that matter.

"These dwarf tale-tellers?" she prompted.

"Yes. Dobbie von Kruse did a very interesting piece on them. They are regarded by the Rom as being a particular repository of the old legends. Rather like those Homeric story-tellers you still find wandering around in Serbia and Croatia. Yet Dobbie could barely scratch the surface, as he found very few of them, and he had to get back to the States before he could record everything he wanted to record. Pity, that." He paused, looking at Edwina as if to sum up her suitability for such a task. "Do you think you might be interested in going out there for a while? I could have a word with some people I know in Washington."

Have a word with some people I know in Washington! Those were exactly the words she wanted to hear, and she rapidly assured him that there was nothing she would like more— nothing—than a field trip to Romania.

"Good," said the professor. "I'll see what I can do."

She took to Bucharest. She had a small flat in a *fin-de-siècle* building overlooking the river, and it was here that she had meetings with the person she described as her facilitator— a hard-up private scholar who had written a history of Romania and who seemed to have good contacts with everybody of any influence in the city and more broadly in the country as a whole. Yes, he could arrange for her to spend time with a Rom family. Yes, he could ensure that they were in touch with one of the elusive dwarf tale-tellers. Yes, he could provide her with such equipment as she required and the transport that would get her to the family's campsite.

Edwina already spoke basic Romanian, having spent six months learning the language before she embarked on the project. It would not be necessary, then, to take an interpreter, as long as the family with whom she was to stay could be persuaded to speak slowly and clearly. There would be no trouble with that, the facilitator assured her, as long as she was prepared to pay them to speak slowly. "These people will do anything for money," he added. She thought that this indicated a somewhat uncharitable view, but she said nothing about it. "One thing you have to remember about Romania," a friend at the United States embassy in Bucharest had warned her, "is not to say anything—to anybody. This place is full of secret agents, of spies, informers, and assassins. You never know who is in the Iron Guard, or in their pay. Most people won't even say good morning to the King, let alone confide in him."

On her first visit to her gypsy community, she was received politely enough by her host—the man wearing the hat and standing in front of the caravan yoke. When she asked him about the dwarf tale-teller, his eyes narrowed. Then he gestured to a nearby bush. "He is lying under a bush at the moment," he said. "It is best not to disturb him just yet."

Anthropologists need to be patient, and so Edwina sat quietly until she saw the foliage of the bush parting and a small, indeed diminutive figure emerge. This small man looked at her for a moment, and then walked over to her host and started a conversation with him. Edwina tried to hear what was said, but could make nothing of it. At length, her host came over and said, "The dwarf is worried that you are unclean."

Edwina frowned. "But I am very particular about that sort of thing," she said. "I had a bath this morning before leaving Bucharest."

"No," said her host. "This is nothing to do with washing. Our people have a strong sense of purity and impurity. I keep explaining it to anthropologists." He sighed. "They don't all get it. We Rom have a concept of pollution that, I'm sorry to say, regards the lower part of the human body as unclean—along with all non-Rom people. So you, I'm afraid, are ranked alongside the lower part of the anatomy. This is not meant to be offensive in any way—it's just the way things are."

Edwina became aware that there was a man wearing a greatcoat standing immediately behind her. He can be seen clearly in the photograph, although his features are obscured by shadow. "Who is that?" she asked her host.

He glanced in the direction of the strange figure. "That is the man from King Carol's secret service," he said. "He is watching you because you are a foreigner—and an American one at that. He will be watching all the time you are here. I shall give him a tarpaulin to sleep under, so that he does not get soaked by the dew."

"Will the dwarf tale-teller tell me some of his traditional stories?" asked Edwina.

The host shook his head. "That will not be possible," he said. "Look at him. He's standing out there in the middle of the field. That is because he thinks you are unclean."

Edwina looked up at the sky. You spent years equipping yourself to investigate the lives of people so different from yourself, and then they turn round and call you unclean. Ungrateful people, ungrateful. And I see no reason why I should pretend to like them. I shall return to Bucharest and write up my report. I shall describe just how awful they are. I shall tell the truth.

She rose. The kettle was never going to boil. In Bucharest they would be serving coffee now, piping-hot and smelling gorgeous. Tonight, she would go out for dinner with some new friends she had made. She no longer cared about the dwarf tale-teller and his people. She was unclean, and unclean people presumably cared very little for those who considered them unclean. Unclean—what a cheek! She would have another bath when she got back to the flat. It would take away the smell of the smoke that had drifted into her clothes. She would luxuriate and then go out and enjoy herself. Why not? Why should anthropologists not have as much fun as others? Why not?

She walked away, leaving the smoking fire, the secret policeman, the tale-teller—leaving all of these people behind. *Bunk,* she muttered under her breath. *Oh, dear Bunk, what are you doing right now, down there in New Orleans? Shall I come and visit you? Yes, I shall. We shall eat crayfish in hot sauce and listen to Dixie and talk about life and other things. Yes, we'll do that, dear Bunk, dear Bunk.*

Duty

CLAIRE AND DOTTY WERE TWINS, separated in their entry into the world by no more than a couple of minutes. The fact that Claire was older than Dotty by those few brief moments determined the shape of both of their lives. When we look in retrospect at the saliences of our lives, we realise, sometimes with astonishment, that this is how they are shaped: a single event; a chance word of advice; an apparently minor decision by another—any of these may dictate what happens to us and what we ourselves do. In the face of this subjection to chance, the role played by free will and what we see as our own choice may seem a small one.

Their parents, Harold and Liza, were pleased with the arrival of twins. Their mother had experienced a difficult pregnancy and the doctor had warned that another could threaten her life. "You have been given two healthy daughters, Mrs. Clarke," he said. "Leave it at that." Harold held Liza's hand and kissed it in gratitude. He could not believe his good fortune, which seemed to him to be unreal, undeserved. "You've given me two girls," he said. "I have you and two lovely girls; that is enough."

A few months later, after a sudden decline in her health, Liza was admitted to hospital in acute pain. An operation was performed, but without success, as Liza died four days later of septicaemia. Harold was left to care for the girls. He was a grocer in Glasgow, who had his own shop and all the cares that that brought. His sister, Peggy, who was a theatre nurse in Manchester, gave up her job to return to Glasgow. She kept house for him and took on responsibility for the twins.

Peggy never questioned the stroke of fate that dictated that she would be destined to look after her brother and his two daughters. In those days, many people, particularly women, shouldered such duties without complaint. Unmarried daughters often stayed at home to look after parents, seeming to accept that this might mean they would have no chance of making their own home with somebody else. The idea that all of us should have the chance of freedom and a life of our own choosing had not yet taken hold, and it did not occur to Peggy, even if she did sometimes reflect on what might have been had Liza not died.

There were few disagreements between Harold and Peggy. "One thing I'd like to make clear, Harold," Peggy said shortly after her return to Glasgow. "I run the house, and that means that what I say goes. Do you understand that, Harold? Do you understand what I'm telling you?"

He was still grieving for Liza and was in no state to argue. And even if he had been, he would not have been inclined to do so. It suited him perfectly that his sister should make these decisions, as he had always yielded that role to Liza. Peggy would simply continue what had gone before.

"You wear the trousers, Peg," Harold said. "My job is to put food on the table. That's all."

"Good," said Peggy. "That suits me very well."

It was Peggy who ruled that the twins should be dressed in matching clothes. "People love that," she said. "They love to see two little children looking identical."

"Do they?" asked Harold. He wondered whether this might not stifle individuality—he was not convinced, when he came to think about it, whether he would care to have been dressed in exactly the same way as his brother. But he did not argue, and became used to the presence on the washing line behind their house of small outfits, always in twos.

It was Peggy, too, who decided that Claire should be told that she was slightly older than her sister. "People need to know these things," she said. "They like to know where they stand."

Harold enquired whether it might not be preferable for them to think of themselves as being exactly the same age. "That way, Claire won't be able to lord it over her sister, you know. They'd be equal-ranking, so to speak."

Peggy gave this view short shrift. "You're wrong, Harold," she said peremptorily. "You're quite wrong on that."

She did not explain further, and Harold did not press the matter. But if Peggy had imagined that telling Claire she was the older sister would not have an effect—and a lasting one at that—then she was the one who was quite wrong. From an early age, Claire asserted her authority. "I'm older than you are," she would say to settle some argument over any of the little things that children argue about—the ownership of a toy, the right to have more of whatever it was that was in short supply, the right to decide what the next game would be.

Dotty seemed to accept this, even if she might argue weakly against her sister's claim. "You're not all that much older," she would say, but without much conviction that this made any difference. "Two minutes is not a long time, Claire."

"It's enough," retorted Claire. "Two minutes is two minutes."

But such disagreements between the sisters were uncommon. They were twins, but they were also the firmest of friends, used to each other's company, and conscious of the fact that they each viewed the world in much the same way. They had other friends, of course, but these friendships were relatively unimportant and, anyway, always depended on the approval of the other sister. If one said of some new acquaintance, "I don't like her all that much," then the other would rapidly agree. "No, you're right," she might say. "I've gone off her, I think."

When they were seven they developed a secret language. This was more than a passing matter, and over the years it developed an extensive vocabulary, along with an elaborate grammar. The words were vaguely Slavic-sounding, as there were many *v* sounds and a large number of the words ended in *-ich*. One of their teachers, overhearing them in the playground, remarked to a colleague, "Those Clarke twins were speaking Serbo-Croat, you know. Maybe that aunt of theirs is Serbian—who would have thought?"

They were happy, although Dotty had about her a slightly melancholic air. She dreamed a lot of her mother, whom she said she could remember—just.

"You can't," said Claire. "Mummy died when we were very little. Tiny."

"But I do," said Dotty. "Because how could I know in my dreams that it's Mummy unless I remembered her a bit? How could I?"

"You're just making her up," Claire replied. "People make up people they don't really know. They think what they might have been like, and then they decide that's how it really was."

"I remember her," Dotty maintained. "She was beautiful. And she was very kind."

Claire at least was prepared to concede that. "Of course she was beautiful. And yes, I think she was kind too."

The twins left school at the age of sixteen and enrolled to train as nurses. They applied to be posted to the same hospital and were given adjoining rooms in the nurses' home. The matron under whom they trained, Matron Russell, looked on them with favour. "Those Clarke girls are hard workers," she said. "They never give any trouble and their work is first class—really first class."

She invited them for tea one day in Matron's Room—a forbidding place to which student nurses were usually bidden only for a dressing-down. They went with some trepidation, but were soon put at ease by Matron, who had bought an iced cake to share with them.

"If the truth be told," Matron Russell said, "I have rather a sweet tooth."

She asked after their father, whom she had met when he had been visiting Liza in hospital. When she disclosed this, Dotty asked, timidly, as if fearful of the answer, "Did you know our mother, Matron?"

Matron Russell nodded. "Yes, I met her. I was a ward sister in those days and I nursed your mother. I remember her well." She paused. "She was a brave woman."

There was silence. Dotty was holding a small piece of iced

cake in her right hand when Matron Russell said this. She involuntarily let a fragment of icing fall to the floor.

"Yes," said Matron Russell. "She was a brave woman. Not everybody's brave, you know. It takes something special to be brave when you know things are not going to end well."

Matron Russell was looking at the small piece of icing on the floor. Dotty reached forward and picked it up, popping it into her mouth.

Matron Russell frowned. "Nurse," she said, "we do not eat from the floor, do we?"

Dotty blushed, and Matron Russell smiled, before adding, "Although I'm pleased that you consider my floor clean enough to eat from."

After they had completed their training, Claire was offered a nursing post in Inverness. She had not applied for this, but had been recommended by Matron Russell, who was friendly with another matron there. Dotty handed her the letter one Saturday when they were having breakfast at home with Harold and Peggy.

"We don't know anybody in Inverness, do we?" she asked, examining the postmark.

Claire slit it open with her table knife, leaving a small line of butter across the flap. "Not a soul," she said.

She read the letter silently, and then looked up at her sister. "I've been offered a job up there. Look." She handed the letter to her sister.

Dotty frowned. "Will you take it? The pay's much higher."

Claire looked out of the window. Harold and Peggy were watching her. Peggy threw Dotty a concerned glance.

"But what about you?" asked Claire at last. "What do you think?"

Harold and Peggy turned to stare expectantly at Dotty.

"Don't mind about me," said Dotty. "You're the oldest. You decide."

Claire took the letter back from Dotty, folding it carefully and replacing it in its envelope. "I don't think so," she said. "Inverness is a long way away."

"An awful long way away," said Harold quickly.

"It's different up there," observed Peggy.

"So you're not going to go?" asked Dotty.

Claire shook her head. "Why go to Inverness?" she asked.

Three weeks later, again on a Saturday, the day off that the twins usually spent at home, a young man with slicked-down hair called at the house. He was the son of somebody with whom Harold had served in the army, and his father had given him the address in order to call upon Harold when he was in Glasgow.

Introductions were made, and Harold announced to the girls, "This is Freddie. His father and I served together." He smiled at the young man. "You look just like your dad, you know. Only his hair was always untidy."

Freddie laughed. "Still is."

Peggy made Freddie a cup of tea and served it with a buttered scone. Freddie drank the tea and ate the scone, which he praised as being delicious. He watched Claire as he spoke, as if addressing all his remarks to her. Dotty saw this. She looked into her teacup.

Freddie called again the next day. He had lost a pocket-book, he claimed, and wondered whether he had left it there. Dotty saw this for the excuse it was.

"We would have seen it if you had left it," she said. "It isn't here."

"I'll search for it," said Claire quickly, looking discouragingly at her sister.

Before he left, Freddie had invited Claire to accompany him to the cinema.

"He's courting you," Dotty said to her sister that evening.

"I know," said Claire. "But he's ever so charming, isn't he?"

Dotty did not reply. She could see what was going to happen. It had a dreadful inevitability to it. Claire would marry Freddie, and she would be left living with their father and aunt. She would have to look after them as they became older. She would never get away—never. And this was all because Claire was older than she was. She thought that gave her the right to have more of a life than her younger sister had.

A few weeks later, Claire said to Dotty that Freddie had introduced her to a friend of his. "He's called William," she said. "He comes from Gourock. He's a butcher. He works in his father's shop. They make meat pies."

"And?"

"And Freddie wonders if you'd like to meet William."

Dotty was silent. Then she said, "Do you think I should? As my older sister, that is? Do you think I should?"

"Yes," said Claire. "You must."

They went to a tea-dance at a local hotel. William was very neat, and he was an accomplished dancer. He taught Dotty a new dance that he said was all the rage "in America and places." At the end of the evening he asked her whether they could meet again the following weekend. She agreed that they could.

"You see," said Claire. "I told you that you'd like him."

Dotty said nothing. She had nothing against William, but she had nothing much for him either. She was in love with Freddie. She had fallen in love with him the moment she had seen him—that first day when he had come round at the suggestion of his father. She wanted nothing more than to be in his company. She imagined what it would be like to be in his arms, and blushed at the shamelessness of her thoughts.

Freddie asked Claire to marry him, and she agreed. A week or two later, William proposed. It was at the end of a number at the local *palais de dance,* and Dotty was drinking a glass of water at the time. She spilled the water, and he laughed. "Does that mean yes?" he asked.

Dotty did not give him a direct answer. She wanted to discuss his proposal with her sister. In fact, she had decided to confess to Claire her feelings for Freddie. She would tell her everything, including the impure thoughts, and then she would offer to go away—to Inverness, perhaps, because there had been nursing jobs advertised there recently and she felt she could get one of those.

"I need to speak to you," she said to Claire. "I need to speak somewhere quiet."

They went into the parlour that Peggy kept for visitors. It smelled of floor polish. There were copies of *The People's Friend* on a small mahogany table.

Her courage failed her. She did not speak about Freddie, but told her sister about William's proposal.

"You must say yes," said Claire.

"But I'm not sure . . ."

Claire shook her head. "Listen, Dotty, William is a good man. He has really good prospects. I'm telling you: Accept him—you may never get another offer as good as that."

Dotty still hesitated.

"I'm telling you as your older sister," Claire said. "Have I ever given you bad advice? Ever?"

Dotty shook her head. "I wonder what Mummy would think," she asked.

"She would be happy," said Claire. "She would be happy for both of us."

Dotty gave William his answer. They were congratulated by Claire and Freddie, who suggested a double wedding.

"You save a lot that way," said Freddie. "And people like it, you know. They love a double wedding."

Preparations were made. Peggy baked tray after tray of tea cakes. Freddie decorated the local church hall, where the reception was to be held. On the day, the two grooms stood up at the head of the church, awaiting their brides. Claire and Dotty came in together, with Harold in between them. His eyes were moist with tears.

They took their places—under their veils, looking neither to left or right—and the minister began.

They were identical twins, and because of this the minister inadvertently married Claire to William and Dotty to Freddie. He noticed his mistake only after the ceremony had finished, and he drew the two couples aside to explain that they would have to go through everything again.

Claire looked at Dotty, and there then passed one of those unspoken moments of communication that only twins experience. Words came at last. "Actually . . . ," began Claire, and Dotty immediately said, "Yes, I've loved him all along—ever since . . ." She did not finish. Claire now said, "And I love William. I didn't want to tell you, but I spoke to him about it."

Dotty was not prepared for this. "You did? And what did he say?"

"He said he felt the same." She paused. "And I think Freddie feels the same about you."

Dotty could scarcely conceal her joy. "He does? Really?"

Claire nodded. She turned to the minister. She was the elder sister, and she acted decisively. "No need to do anything," she said. "We're happy with things the way they are."

They lived contented lives, for the most part. Dotty had twins herself—two boys—both of whom went to live in Australia. She wrote to them, *Be sure to live your own lives, boys. One day you might know what I mean, but in the meantime make that a rule for yourselves.*

One of the boys wrote back, *You're right, Ma. Too right.*

Iron Jelloids

WHAT THE ADVERTISING AGENCY said to the Thomas Middleby Talent Company was quite clear. *We act,* they wrote, *for a well-known iron tonic manufacturer. Their product, Iron Jelloids, will no doubt be known to you (although we are not suggesting, of course, that you yourselves are in need of a tonic of this nature!).*

This caused smiles at the Talent Company, where the proprietor, Thomas Middleby, did, in fact, occasionally take Iron Jelloids at the behest of his wife. "She swears by them," he said. "She tells me you can never have enough iron. Never."

We are preparing, the agency continued, *a newspaper advertisement that will be placed in the national and local press over the forthcoming winter. For this we need two models, one female and one male. These are not to be glamorous people: the woman should be of presentable appearance, the sort with whom female teachers and young (but respectable) married women may readily identify. There are more specific requirements for the male model: he must be shorter than the woman and rather inadequate in his appearance. He should, in essence, be one who looks as if he could benefit from the general enhancement that our client's product undoubtedly supplies. We trust that you will be able to provide persons for our photographic session in a fortnight's time. We shall furnish costumes, which will be those of a tram inspector and a conductress. Please bear in mind that we are not seeking to engage Jeanette MacDonald and Nelson Eddy!*

"Well," said Thomas Middleby, "there's no doubt about what they're looking for."

His assistant smiled. "Merlin?" he asked.

Thomas nodded. "You read my mind."

His assistant consulted a red ledger on the table in front of him. "I hardly need to look," he said. "When did Merlin last get a booking? Can you even remember?"

"He did something for the Public Health people," said Thomas. "That advertisement on the dangers of an inadequate diet in childhood. Remember?"

The assistant rolled his eyes. "They said he was perfect. They said that the advertisement worked. They had a lot of people writing in and asking whether daily malt would help their children not to look like Merlin when they grew up. It was a big success."

Thomas agreed. He had sometimes described Merlin as the runt of their litter—a man so perfectly unprepossessing that he could enter a room with a fanfare and still not be noticed. There was a need for such models, of course—not everybody wanted film-star looks and a bearing to match; but, at the same time, not everyone wanted somebody quite as *mousey* as Merlin. That was why Merlin had few bookings, and it was probably also the reason why he refused to acknowledge that he would never get very far in his modelling career. "Mousey people often just fail to get it," said Thomas. "Everybody else understands, but they don't. It goes with being mousey, perhaps. You don't realise just how . . . how insignificant you really are."

They sent a telegram to Merlin. *National agency planning*

major campaign. Stop. Report to office soonest. Stop. Middleby Talent.

He responded immediately, arriving at the office the following morning, dressed in a grey suit with velvet strips on the cuffs and around the pockets. Thomas was convinced that this had come from a theatrical outfitters, as he was sure he had seen it in an Oscar Wilde play, but he had not expressed his doubts.

"Merlin," he said, "I have something big for you. Really big."

Merlin tried not to seem too keen. "I'll take a look at it," he said. And then, after a suitable pause, added, "Tell me more."

Thomas explained about the Iron Jelloids campaign. He did not mention their stipulation that the man should be mousey; he referred, rather, to the *male lead,* a term suggestive of matinées and the idols who appeared in them. Merlin was not slow to appreciate the reference, and glowed with pleasure.

"I'll look at the diary," he said, once Thomas had finished.

Thomas suppressed a smile. "It's really important," he said. "I know how busy you are, but I would appreciate a quick response."

Merlin was magnanimous. "All right," he said. "I can always cancel something else. I'll take the job."

"That's uncommonly good of you, Merlin," said Thomas. "I'll let them know that they can book the shoot."

"Who will be the female lead?" asked Merlin.

Thomas consulted his papers. "A young woman called Estelle Harbord. She's much in demand, but I think we can get her. She's charming, and I'm sure you two will work well together."

This was true. Estelle's complexion was such that she was often asked to pose for soap advertisements. "Milky soft," muttered one photographer. "The sort of face a cat would love to lick."

Merlin went back to his lodgings. He occupied a room in the house of a police sergeant's widow. The widow, Mrs. Sullivan, was fond of Merlin, who had stayed in her house for over two years now. She had given him the room at the back, where it was quieter, and had gone to some lengths to make it as attractive and cheerful as possible. It had fresh red curtains and a chintz-covered armchair. On the wall there was an engraving of a rural scene—a shepherd with his two dogs—and an ornately framed picture of the Sacred Heart, as both Mrs. Sullivan and Merlin were Catholics. "I'm not Irish, though," Merlin occasionally said. "Don't get me wrong on that."

Mrs. Sullivan had been most helpful to Merlin. When he had first taken the room, she had introduced him to a man who owned a betting shop. "I don't really approve of gambling," she said, "but Mr. Todd runs a very orderly establishment and has given more than generously to the League of Mary. He tells me that he needs a part-time clerk and bookkeeper and that he would be prepared to train you if you wanted the position."

The job suited Merlin very well, as the hours were flexible and enabled him to continue with his modelling career.

Most of the time there were no modelling contracts, and he was able to put in a good number of hours in the betting shop, where he was popular with Mr. Todd's secretary and the cleaner. They called him *Ducky*, which he interpreted as a term of affection; in reality, although they concealed this, it was a nickname based on the way he walked, which reminded them of a duck's gait. "Heaven knows what they want him to model," said the secretary. "Poor Ducky!"

"Likely as not he's the *before* in one of those *before and after* advertisements," said the cleaner. "I'll look out for him in the magazines."

Mrs. Sullivan would have given short shrift to such comments, had she heard them. She was fiercely protective of Merlin. She had her hopes for him, and had said to more than one of her friends that if there was any justice in this world he would meet a pleasant and companionable woman and settle down to married life. "He would not be a troublesome husband," she said. "He would be . . . how should one put it? He would be a good man to have in the background, so to speak."

Her friends saw what she meant, but had their doubts. "The problem," said one of them, "is that Merlin is too mild. Now, there's nothing wrong with *some* mildness in a man, but most women want something with a bit more . . . a bit more . . ." She strained to find the right expression. Vigour? Iron, perhaps?

Mrs. Sullivan did not think along those lines. She felt that it was only a matter of time before a suitable woman would come along and would see Merlin's finer points: his readiness to listen rather than to speak, for example, his way of drinking tea without slurping—a small but important point—and his general attentiveness. Merlin was always ready to do the washing up, and was more than happy to go off on errands to the grocer if the weather was inclement and Mrs. Sullivan felt inclined to stay in front of the fire.

She made several attempts at introductions, but none of these worked. On one occasion the woman reported back to her after Merlin had invited her to tea at a corner house. "Oh dear," she said. "There were long silences. I tried my best, you know, but it was heavy going. I don't like to be fussy, but I must say I would far prefer to meet a man with a bit of *oomph* in him. Sorry about that."

Mrs. Sullivan understood. "I can see what you mean," she said. "I take the view, though, that there's a really good nature there and that these things you're looking for . . ."

"Strength, for one," suggested her friend.

"All right, strength—that might come with time."

"I doubt it," said the friend.

Mrs. Sullivan, of course, was pleased to hear about the planned photo-shoot for Iron Jelloids. She listened as Merlin told her of the instructions he had received from the agency. "They want to do photographs in which I am seen with a well-known actress called Estelle Harbord. You'll probably have heard of her."

"No," said Mrs. Sullivan. "Never. But that's not to say she's not well known."

"She was in a Gilbert and Sullivan show once," said Merlin. "The chorus. *The Mikado*."

"I'd like to say I'm related to that Sullivan," said Mrs. Sullivan. "But I'm not, I'm afraid."

"And I have no connection with the court of King Arthur," said Merlin.

They both laughed. Then Mrs. Sullivan asked, "Have you ever tried these Iron Jelloids?"

Merlin shook his head. "Can't say I have."

Mrs. Sullivan thought for a moment before continuing, "You should try them. I have some in the bathroom cabinet. Let me get them for you."

Merlin read what was written on the packet. "It says they are a reliable tonic. It says that they give you more strength and energy."

"They're very effective in those departments," said Mrs. Sullivan. "If I ever feel a bit below par, I take them for a few days and I feel much invigorated. They really work."

Merlin fingered the packet. "I don't know," he began. "I'm not sure whether . . ."

"There's no harm in trying them," said Mrs. Sullivan. "They don't taste bad and they are very good at combating anaemia. You're perfectly welcome to try them—I have more somewhere or other."

Merlin took an Iron Jelloid out of the packet and popped it into his mouth. "I can taste the iron," he said. "I really can."

"There you are," said Mrs. Sullivan. "They do what they claim to do."

By arrangement with the tram company, the Iron Jelloids photo-shoot took place during a quiet time at their depot on the edge of town. A retired tram driver had been recruited to move the tram to a position where the light would be just right, and he reminisced at length with the photographer about his early days on the trams. The shoot director, a young man in a coat with fur trim on the collar, looked anxiously at his watch. It was a cold day and the weather forecast had warned of snow showers; they needed to begin.

While being dressed in a vacant tram office, Estelle had asked the wardrobe mistress whether she knew Merlin. "Who is he?" she asked. "They haven't told me anything about him."

The wardrobe mistress took a pin out of her mouth. "Nobody," she said. "He's nobody."

Estelle smiled. "He must be *somebody*," she said.

"He's a funny wee fellow," said the other woman. "He's slightly cross-eyed. There's not much to him. If the wind came up, it would probably blow him away."

Estelle said nothing. She loved modelling and the theatre, but she did not like the sharpness of the tongues she encountered there. There was a lot of failure in that world, she thought, and it was their own failure that made people bitter.

"I look forward to meeting him," she muttered, glancing at her reflection in a mirror held by the wardrobe mistress. "Do I look like a real conductress?"

"Perfect. And may I say something else, Estelle? Your skin is really beautiful. It really is. The last time I saw a complexion like yours it was on a duchess. No, I'm not making that up. I saw a duchess in the flesh—a very young one—and she had a complexion just like yours." She paused. "Some people have all the luck, you know—even if they don't deserve it."

They went outside, where Merlin, already in his tram inspector's costume, was waiting for Estelle. They were introduced by the shoot director, who, after making the introductions, said, "All right, everybody—this is the story. Boy has met girl. Not much chance for him, I'm afraid, because he's pretty weedy. But . . . and here's the selling point, everybody, he's been taking Iron Jelloids, and now, guess what, he has more confidence. He's stronger. He doesn't feel like a shorty any longer. He proposes to her, on the step of the tram. And underneath the photograph of this touching little encounter we'll have the words: *Now that I'm taking Iron Jelloids I feel I can at last propose!*" He paused. "Got it?" he asked.

Estelle nodded. Merlin looked away. Then Estelle mounted the step of the tram, and that is when it happened.

It took place very quickly, as most accidents do. The driver of the tram had been in the cab, but stepped out because he believed a brake was on. It was not, and when he left the controls the tram, which was on a very slight slope, started to roll backwards. The photographer shouted out, and the driver was alerted. He started back to the cab, but tripped, and fell heavily on the ground. On the step of the tram, Estelle hung on to a railing and uttered a shriek.

Without hesitation, Merlin sprang forward and put his shoulder to the side of the tram in an attempt to stop its motion. Of course, it was an impossible task, but for a second or two it seemed that he was impeding it. And during those seconds, the driver stumbled to his feet and climbed back into the cab to apply the brake.

"Oh, my goodness!" exclaimed the director. "Talk about an action shot!"

"Are you all right?" Estelle asked Merlin solicitously. "You were a real hero there."

"Perfectly all right," Merlin replied, dusting the side of his jacket. And then, with a shaft of wit, asked the director, "Was that in the contract?"

They all laughed.

"Back to work!" shouted the director, clapping his hands.

That evening, Mrs. Sullivan listened as Merlin related the events of the day. She was particularly interested to hear about Estelle Harbord.

"We got on very well," said Merlin. "We have a lot in common."

Mrs. Sullivan hardly dared ask the question. It was the most important question of all in her view. "Is she Catholic?" she asked.

Merlin smiled. "I don't see what difference that makes."

Mrs. Sullivan looked away. "You know what I mean, Merlin. You know full well."

He sighed. "You're as bad as my mother sometimes, Mrs. Sullivan. But yes, the answer's yes."

"That's nice." She paused. "Will you be seeing her again, do you think?"

She knew what the answer would be. Estelle Harbord would be well above poor Merlin's station. It was unfair—so unfair.

"As it happens," he said, "we shall be going out together tomorrow."

"Oh, I'm so glad you asked her," said Mrs. Sullivan.

"She asked me," said Merlin.

"My goodness."

Merlin sat back in his chair. He felt so good. He felt confident. He felt strong. This was it—there was no doubt about it. He was good at reading people's expressions, and he had read Estelle's without difficulty. She had fallen for him—she definitely had.

And he was right. She had. They married six months later. At the wedding service, Mrs. Sullivan felt a greater joy than she had ever experienced before, even at her own wedding. This, she thought, is an expression of the Holy Spirit, beyond any doubt—and Iron Jelloids too, she said to herself, guilty at the very thought.

Students

I AM VERY, VERY CROSS, and I think my discontent is evident in this photograph. People always tell you to smile when you are having your photograph taken, but sometimes that is just too much to ask. This was such an occasion. I simply could not smile because a smile would have been completely wrong in the circumstances. I did not feel like smiling. Definitely not.

Let me tell you a little bit about myself. My name is Alfred George Morrison and I am forty-seven years old. People say that I look a bit older; that, I suppose, is because of all the responsibilities I have to shoulder, particularly when it comes to my wife's relatives, some of whom, I am sorry to say, are downright feckless. I know that is an inflammatory thing to say, but I see no way round it. Either one says nothing or one says something like that. Fecklessness cannot be buried under the carpet. Fecklessness will inevitably come out.

My wife, of course, is an exception. She is hard-working and utterly reliable. She is quite unlike her two sisters, their husbands, and their various offspring, particularly one Henry William Maxwell, a student—or so he claims. I have never seen him with a book, however, and I very much doubt whether he possesses one. I shall say more about this young man shortly.

My wife, Susan Patricia Morrison, née Maxwell, comes from Stranraer. I come from Dunfermline, and have lived most of my life in Fife. I see no reason to go anywhere else—

certainly I wouldn't care to go to Stranraer. It's not that I have anything against my wife's home town, other than her relatives, that is.

But I should start at the beginning, I suppose. My father was a butcher. He started with a small shop in Dunfermline, but after a while bought another one, and another one after that. He soon had shops in Perth, Dundee, and Aberdeen. There were smaller shops in places like Forfar and Montrose. He was one of the most successful butchers in Scotland and was even chosen as Scottish Businessman of the Year by the Dundee *Courier*. He was very proud of that, and the issue in which this award was announced was framed on the wall behind his desk. I now have that and keep it in a prominent position in our house, along with my father's curling trophies, of which there are six. He said to me once, "If we were to have another ice age, Alfred, it would be a great thing for curling." My father was very witty, and he often said things like that—observations that were thoroughly original and yet could bring a smile to the lips.

My father could have sent me off to an expensive school—to Dollar Academy, or somewhere like that—but he did not, and I am glad that he did not. I received the same schooling as everybody else, and so nobody can point at me and say that I got where I am by virtue of a privileged start. "You're learning exactly the same as everybody else, Alfred," my father said. "Namely, almost nothing."

He could have made life easy for me, but he realised that this would not give me the best start. Things that you have not achieved yourself are always less rewarding than the things you have earned through your own hard work. All I ever received from my father was a gift of four thousand pounds when I turned twenty-one—and a share in the shops, of course. But that came later, and by that time I had already built up my own business.

Four thousand pounds is a lot of money, and I went to see my father's bank manager to discuss what to do with it.

"Gilts," he said. "I always recommend gilts. Put the money there and it's safe. It has the Government behind it."

"But what about capital growth?" I asked. I had read somewhere that with gilts you got back only the face value.

"They are perhaps not the best investment for capital growth," the bank manager conceded. "But is that what you want?"

It was.

"In that case," the manager said, "buy property. You can't go wrong with property." He paused. "Well, you can, actually. I've known people who find their house is not worth as much as they think. You can pay too much for property, you see. And then you have to insure it, and there are the rates and repairs and . . . well, property is not for everybody, I suppose. But I can still recommend it if you want security."

Acting on this advice, I purchased a number of small houses in Perth, Dundee, and St. Andrews. The houses in this photograph were my properties in St. Andrews, in a small street on the edge of the town. They were in reasonable condition when I bought them, although the plumbing in all of them left something to be desired. I found a good plumber, though— a hard-working man who was an elder of the local church—

and he made a fine job of the refurbishment I undertook. I also secured the services of a conscientious house-painter and a skilled joiner. With all these men working on them, the houses were soon in a suitable condition to be let to tenants.

Then I made my mistake. Instead of letting the houses on the open market, I foolishly listened to an approach from my wife's younger sister, Ethel, whose son, Henry, was enrolling for a course at St. Andrews University. I had met this young man on several occasions, and although I did not like him very much, I had not heard that he was at all troublesome. In spite of my reservations, I agreed to let the house to him, to live in during the four years of his degree course. He then asked me if his friends could have the lease of the two houses next door. These friends, like him, were all beginning their studies at the university and needed to find somewhere to live.

"They're sound chaps, Uncle," Henry said. "There's Eddie Wilson, who also comes from Stranraer, and Bob Anderson, from Glasgow. They'll be sharing with a few friends, but all of them, I can assure you, will be reliable tenants."

"How do you know these people?" I asked.

"From rugby," he said. "We've all played in the same team over the last few years."

"Will they look after the place?"

Henry assured me they would. "I've played alongside Eddie in the scrum, Uncle. You get to know people at close quarters in the scrum. You can tell what they're like."

I saw his point. I have never played rugby myself, but I know some people who have, and they tend to be respectable, trustworthy people, even if not very bright. But you can't have everything, can you? If you are given a talent for rugby, then that's something worth having. I cannot play rugby, but I must admit, although I don't say this too openly, I am probably fairly near the top when it comes to intellect. I hope that this does not sound like boasting—it's not; it is simply being realistic. "No point in hiding your light under a bus," my father used to say. I found this very funny, as the original expression is *hiding your light under a bushel*. I understood the joke, although there were many who did not. That's the problem with subtlety; not everyone gets it. There is no credit in pretending to be stupid if you clearly are not.

I had a niggling doubt about Henry, as I did about all my wife's relatives, and had I listened to these doubts, I would not have agreed to let the houses to him and his friends. However, as the expression goes, it is no use crying over spilled milk.

The first weekend after the students moved in, they had a party. I was in Dunfermline that weekend, and it was not until Sunday afternoon that I received a telephone call from the plumber.

My plumber is in the same Masonic lodge as I am. Perhaps I should not be telling you this, as the whole point about being a member of a secret society is that you don't reveal who is in it. We Masons do not like the term *secret society,* as it suggests an organisation that gets up to no good. That is definitely not what we are about; we are about doing things for the benefit of others, particularly for the benefit of other Masons. And what is wrong with that? If you don't look after your friends, then who will you look after? Of course, people will say that Masons will give their friends preference when it comes to handing out jobs. Once again, what exactly is wrong with that? If you know that somebody is a Mason, then you can be assured that he will be a hard-working, reliable man. That is more or less guaranteed.

There are many advantages to being a Mason, and I shall give you an example. Some time ago, there was a man who was charged with a serious financial fraud. He was put on trial at the High Court in Glasgow, and he found himself in front of a jury of fifteen random citizens. We have fifteen jurors in Scotland, rather than twelve, as is the case in England. Our system is better, of course, as most things Scottish are a bit better once you start to look closely. This is not to run down England—I have great respect for England and the English—but they could well do to take a leaf out of Scotland's book in many areas of life, including the law.

This man found himself in the High Court and was understandably quite intimidated. But when he looked at the jurors, he was delighted to see that there were several members who looked as if they might be Masons. So he made the secret sign fairly early on in the proceedings, and I'm happy to say that the jurors returned it. They were discreet about it, of course, as one does not want to publicise these things. And for that reason I shall not tell you what it was.

But there was something else. The judge happened to be looking in his direction when he made the sign, and the judge himself made a Masonic sign. That was the icing on the cake as far as the accused was concerned.

Now, you may be wondering what happened. Well, I'm sorry to say that the jury found him guilty. There was a lot of evidence, you see. And then, when it came to the sentencing, the judge gave him the stiffest sentence at his disposal. It transpired that the judge was not a Mason after all—the sign that he had been thought to be giving was really just a movement preparatory to blowing his nose. These things are easily confused. But the story does go to show that Masons are honest men and will not bend the law. That story should be told to our critics, most of whom, I suspect, are only critical because nobody has ever asked them to be Masons.

But back to our plumber. He said to me over the phone, "I happened to be passing those places of yours. You let them to students, didn't you?"

I told him that this was so.

"Bad idea," he said.

There was a silence down the line—a silence that can only be described as ominous.

"Has something happened?" I asked.

"It looks as if they've had a party," the plumber said. "I think you should come over and check up on things."

I lost no time in driving from Dunfermline to St. Andrews. The sight that met my eyes was quite shocking. There had definitely been a party—in all three houses.

There was no door left to knock on, and so I went straight in. Henry was in the living room, and he greeted me enthusiastically.

"Uncle!" he said. "This really is an unexpected pleasure. Will you stay for a cup of tea?"

It took me some time to recover the ability to speak. When I did, I uttered what I imagine sounded like a strangled cry.

"Are you all right, Uncle?" Henry enquired. "I suppose the place is a bit untidy, but we'll soon sort that out. The chaps had a party last night. The Rugby Club. It went on a bit late, I'm afraid." He smiled, and then continued, "But I've got some good news for you."

I waited.

"Molly came to the party," he said.

I caught my breath. My daughter Molly was training as a nurse in Dundee. She lived in a nurses' residence there—a well-supervised place—and I had not imagined that she went to parties in St. Andrews.

"Molly's engaged," said Henry. "I thought you might like to know. I imagine that she'll tell you later on today. She's gone back to Dundee. Work, I think."

I opened my mouth to say something, but no sound came.

"Yes," Henry continued. "She and Eddie—you know, Eddie Wilson—have decided to get engaged. Last night's party was a bit about that, I suppose. Everybody was really pleased. Eddie's from Stranraer, you know."

I sat down, but the chair broke.

"Sorry about that," said Henry. "Eddie was standing on it last night. Maybe he's a bit on the heavy side. He's a prop, you know—he's going to be playing for the university this season."

Picking myself up from the floor, I confronted Henry in all my outrage. He stared at me, and, when I had finished, looked about him with an air of complete insouciance. "But Uncle," he said, "we'll tidy up. There's no need to blow a gasket."

And then he had the effrontery—the sheer, naked effrontery—to make a Masonic sign to me. He had obviously picked it up from somewhere, as I can't imagine any self-respecting lodge would ever admit him as a member.

I was outraged. "It's no good pulling your left ear-lobe like that," I shouted. "That will do you no good at all."

"Maybe it should have been the right ear-lobe," Henry said. "Sorry."

I left and drove straight down to Dundee. Molly was at work, but I went to the hospital and demanded to see her.

"I've got really good news," she said as she came out of the ward. "Eddie Wilson and I are engaged. He's going to ask you tomorrow, he said. I told him that you'd have no objection."

I started to cry.

"But, Daddy," said Molly, putting an arm about my shoulder. "You mustn't cry. I'm still your little girl and you'll really like Eddie. I know you will."

It took three weeks for the houses to be rendered habitable again. As a result of my wife's intervention, Henry and his friends were allowed to stay, subject to a stern warning that there were to be no further parties or, if there were, no members of the Rugby Club were to be invited. Henry gave me his word that this condition would be scrupulously observed.

Molly also made representations. Could Eddie live rent-free, since he was now family—or almost? I had no alternative but to agree.

"It's very generous of you, Mr. Morrison," said Eddie, with a broad smile. "Or should I call you Dad?"

Zeugma

S HE IS SMILING, the young woman perched on the cross-bar; she is smiling broadly as they follow the tram lines. Behind them, the morning mist is lifting slowly, although the figures within it are ghost-like and the trees still harbour lingering pockets of darkness.

She did not know what possessed her to accept a ride into work from Professor Mactaggart. She barely knew him, although she had seen him in the library, of course, when he came in to request a book from the special collection, or to trace an obscure reference to the work of some philologist nobody had ever heard of. He was always dressed in the same way, even in the summer, when everybody else changed into lighter clothes. Seemingly indifferent to the change in the seasons, he would wear the same heavy overcoat, the same dark thorn-proof suit, and the same flat cap. The head librarian was scathing about the cap. "A professor shouldn't wear something like that," he said, his nasal voice full of disapproval. "Who does he think he is? A golfer?"

Amanda, the young woman, thought the head librarian very stuffy. Why should a professor of English language ("I'm really just a grammarian," he said) not wear a flat cap if that was what he wanted to do? Did it somehow detract from his status? She thought not, and would not particularly care even if it did. Professor Mactaggart was a distinguished scholar—everybody knew that—and if he chose to wear inappropriate clothes, then that was his prerogative. People talked too much anyway—they sniped at those who were a little bit different in their mannerisms or appearance; they ridiculed anybody who did not quite fit in. What was the point of that? Was dull uniformity really what they wanted? Imagine, she said to herself, what it would be like if everybody were to be like the head librarian.

The professor had stopped, just as she turned the corner of the road where she lived with her parents and her younger sister, Jane. Jane was a student nurse who was not sure of her vocation. "Bedpans, bedpans, bedpans," she complained. Amanda had pointed out that there must be more than that to nursing. "Wiping brows," she said. "Taking temperatures. Holding people's hands when they're really ill. What about all that? That must be rewarding enough, surely?"

"I suppose so," said Jane.

Now the professor came along, his bicycle rattling over the cobblestones.

"Miss . . ." He had forgotten her name. That was not surprising; few of the professors bothered to learn the names of the junior staff.

"From the library," she said. "The issue desk."

That would be enough, she thought. But he persisted, "Miss . . . ?"

"Thwaites," she said. "Miss Thwaites."

"Of course. Of course."

He dismounted. "It occurred to me," he said, "that we are going in the same direction, you and I. You will be going to the library, and, as it happens, that's where I'm planning to call in before I go off to my room in college."

She waited. She noticed that there were beads of perspiration on his brow and on his upper lip. Jane might have wiped them away with all her nurse's assurance, but she could not.

"I was wondering," the professor continued, "whether you would care for a lift."

She looked at him in puzzlement.

"I mean, on the bar of my bicycle," he explained. "It's not the most comfortable mode of transport—I'll give you that—but it'll save you a long walk."

She had accepted, without really knowing why she had done so. She did not mind the walk to work, as it gave her the exercise that she felt she needed. And yet, if a professor—and a renowned one at that—should offer to give you a lift on his bicycle, surely you should accept.

He had shown her where to sit. "Don't lean to either side," he said. "That would destabilise us. Just look straight ahead."

They set off rather faster than she would have liked, but she soon got used to the bicycle's particular motion—and its centre of gravity. Out on the main road, after crossing the tramlines, they made their way towards the university—a cluster of spires in the distance. A church bell rang the half hour somewhere, and then another, sounding through the last of the mist.

"Are you comfortable enough?" asked the professor.

She giggled. "Sort of. Actually, no—I'm not all that comfortable, but it's all right."

"It won't take long," he said. "Do you know the song? 'A Bicycle Built for Two'? Do you know it?"

"Of course."

He swerved slightly. "Daisy—the young lady in that song—was happy enough on their tandem. She had a proper seat, of course." He paused, and then he said, rather loudly, "Bearing in mind that neither of us had really planned this, one might perhaps say: *She was carried into town on a cross-bar and a whim.*"

She smiled. And that is the smile we see in the photograph.

But then the professor continued, "*On a cross-bar and a whim.* Do you know what that is?"

She shook her head.

"It's a zeugma," said the professor. "It's a well-known figure of speech. The classic example is *She went straight home, in a flood of tears and a sedan chair.* That's Dickens, no less."

"So that's a zeugma?"

"Yes. It's a figure of speech. It makes one want to smile."

She could see that.

"Because," the professor continued, "there's a contrast be-tween the two elements in the sentence." He paused. "Forgive me if I sound pedantic."

She assured him that he did not. "I'm interested," she said.

"The essence of a zeugma is the contrast between a literal expression and a metaphor. So in the example of the sedan chair, being in a sedan chair is not a metaphor, but being in a flood of tears is. We're not talking about a real flood, are we? That's a metaphor."

"I see."

"And so, in our first example, we have *on a cross-bar,* and *on a whim,* which is metaphorical. To act on a whim is more metaphorical than literal."

She looked into the dark foliage of the trees off to their right. He noticed the direction of her gaze.

"Leafy bowers," he said. "That's a concealed metaphor because bowers were originally rooms. Then they became shady places. There's a concealed metaphor there."

They continued their ride. The sun had broken through now, and was warm upon her face.

"The Greeks had a much broader concept of metaphor," said the professor. "I tell my students to go off and read Aristotle on the subject. He's very enlightening."

"Oh yes?"

"Yes. I often go back to Aristotle, you know. He said there are three important features of metaphor: *saphes,* which means lucidity—lovely word that, Miss . . ."

"Thwaites."

"Of course, Miss Thwaites. *Lucidity. Lambent:* that's another lovely word. Look at the light behind us—no, don't turn around—but look at it when we reach our destination. Such a lovely, soft light. Lambent."

She looked ahead. The light was on the damp cobblestones. It was silver. "And then? The other things about metaphor?"

"There's *saphes,* which is the state of being clear. That's a very special state, which some people, and some expressions, simply do not have. And then there's *xenikon,* which is strangeness. A metaphor must be strange—it must make us sit up and take notice in a way in which a literal expression does not."

The professor stopped talking. She looked out towards the canal, which was on the other side of the road, away to their left. A crew was rowing on the river, the young men bent over their oars, moving in hunched rhythm.

"Do you know," the professor began, "there was a boat on the river called the *Zeugma*? Did you know that?"

He seemed to expect an answer. "No," she said. And then added, "Who would have thought."

"Exactly," said the professor. "It was an odd sort of boat—a little steamer, with a very small chimney. They kept the coal at the back."

"I wonder if it's still there," she said.

"I've looked out for it," said the professor. "I don't always pay much attention to boats, but I'd like to see the *Zeugma* again. It appeals to me as a grammarian, I suppose."

"There might be a boat called the *Metaphor*," she said. "It would be a boat only in a metaphorical sense, and so I wouldn't care to embark on her. A purely metaphorical boat might not actually float."

The professor laughed. "Oh, my goodness," he said. "What a wonderful image. A metaphorical boat, going down under the weight of its symbolism. Hah!"

He turned the bicycle, and for a few moments they wobbled precariously. But she resisted the temptation to lean, and they were quickly righted. Now they were in sight of the library, and the professor steered the bicycle to the side of the road. There he lowered a leg to stabilise them, and then dismounted. Giving her his hand, he helped her off the cross-bar.

"I usually park my cycle right here," he said. "On days that I come to the library, I lean it against this tree."

He bent down to take the cycle clips off his trouser legs.

Standing up again, he looked at her. She thought: Now he looks so sad.

"Are you sure you're all right?" she asked.

He nodded. "Yes, I am. I'm quite all right."

"It's just that you looked . . . well, forgive me, you looked a bit sad."

He hesitated. "Well, I am, I suppose. A touch sad."

"Is there anything . . ."

He did not let her finish. "It's kind of you, but I don't think there's anything anyone can do. I was thinking of my son, you see. Every so often, I think of him. Every day, in fact. Every day."

And then she knew; she knew immediately.

"Oh, I'm so sorry. I'm so, so sorry."

"He fell two days before the Armistice. It was that close, that close."

She did not say anything. She had learned, through experience, that there were times when nothing could be said.

He was looking away. "Over the top," he said, "and overcome." He paused. "Another zeugma, I fear." He tried to smile; he tried.

She reached out and took his hand again. A small flock of pigeons flew past, a flutter of wings, silent in their flight; but then, from another place, birdsong, farther and farther . . . all the birds of Oxfordshire and Gloucestershire, she thought, as another had said, who had also gone. *Yes, I remember Adlestrop.* That poem. The words came back to her.

"All the birds . . . ," she began.

And he said, ". . . of Oxfordshire and Gloucestershire. Yes."

Urchins

F ROM LEFT TO RIGHT: Willy Henderson (lying down), Graham Davie (with box on head), Tommy White (leaning against crate), Johnny Soutar (in toorie), Wee Jimmy Edwards (striding out), Mac Burns (seated on pavement), Norrie Burns (leaning against wall), and Martin Henderson (also leaning).

Look first at Johnny Soutar. He seems pensive, as if trying to weigh something up.

His father was an engine driver, who was born in Perth in 1888. His mother was Irish, a dressmaker who took in repair work to help support her six children. His father died of tuberculosis. He said to the minister who visited him in hospital, "I've done my best by my bairns." And the minister said, "I know that, Thomas. I know."

These are Johnny's boots:

Boots were passed from child to child, sometimes being sixth- or seventh-hand. These would serve no child after Johnny, barely seeing him through to the winter. They were parish boots, public boots made available to children of poor families.

This photograph was taken in 1920, when Johnny was nine. In 1939, Johnny was twenty-eight and a welder in an engineering works in Clydebank, when he joined the army, signing up in the 51st Highland Division. He acquired a reputation as a fighter and was often on a charge. His Regimental Sergeant Major, however, understood him, and said that for all his faults you could always rely on Johnny Soutar.

He landed with the 51st in Sicily and fought his way across the island. One of his officers was a man called Hamish Henderson, who wrote words to accompany that haunting pipe tune "Farewell to the Creeks." Years later, when Johnny heard Hamish singing it in Sandy Bell's Bar in Edinburgh, he wept openly. *All the bricht chaumers are empty . . .* He remembered the echoing emptiness of the barrack rooms left behind. He saw the crowds of women, children, men—all relieved at the end of their nightmare and the arrival of the liberators. He saw a woman come out to throw her arms around him and kiss him. There was wine on her breath. She was in tears.

Johnny married a young woman from Dunoon. They had three children, one of whom went to Glasgow University and became a marine engineer. Johnny died in 1974. George Macleod spoke at his funeral and called him a fine man who was a credit to Scotland. A piper played "Farewell to the Creeks" and people then adjourned to a local hotel, where tea and sandwiches were served. That was the life of Johnny Soutar—not much, perhaps, but he played his part in the freeing of the world from a frightening tyranny. He asked no thanks for that; expected no plaudits.

"You're an awfie wee actor, Willy Henderson," they said. "One of these days folk are going to take you seriously and then what?"

But Willy was incorrigible. His favourite trick was to surprise people by playing dead. Sometimes he would do this around corners so that people would suddenly come across a supine figure, eyes closed, on the pavement at their feet. They would not see Willy watching them through a crack in his eyelids, struggling to keep a straight face. On a number of occasions an ambulance would be called and would arrive, bell clanging, to find an embarrassed member of the public struggling to explain what had happened. "There was a wee boy right there," they would say. "Right there. I thought he was deid. Then up he gets and hares off."

"Willy Henderson," said the ambulance men. "That wee devil. We'll tan his hide if we ever lay hands on him."

At eighteen, Willy Henderson found a job as a stage hand. By a stroke of good luck, he was given a small part in a pantomime after a flu epidemic depleted the cast. He acted with Harry Gordon, who played the Laird of Inversneaky, and with Stanley Baxter. He was never happy.

"I want to play Hamlet," he said.

People thought that a joke, but he meant it.

He never married. There was a woman in the background, people said. She came from somewhere in the Far East—the Philippines, some opined; others were sure it was Thailand.

He lived in a flat in which he grew bonsai trees.

Graham Davie carried a box on his head. He always wore the same cap, several sizes too big for him, and he would rest

the bottom of the box on that. "Your lugs keep your cap on and your cap keeps your box on," Willy Henderson said. "If you took away your lugs, the whole thing would collapse."

These are his shoes, which were passed down to him from his two brothers.

Nobody knew what Graham carried in the box. Some said that it was a body; others said that it was money. One day, the box disappeared. Graham refused to discuss the matter.

"Where's that box of yours, Graham?"

He looked away, and declined to answer.

Graham joined the merchant navy. In 1942, the ship he was serving on was torpedoed in the North Atlantic. He survived the attack, although his chest never recovered from ingested oil. He opened a bar in Gourock and became a member of the Labour Party. "Everything we have," he said, "we've had to fight for. Fight, fight, fight. Nothing comes to you without effort."

John Smith, the leader of the Labour Party, said of him, "Graham didn't know the answer to all the important questions, but my God, he knew the questions to ask."

This is Martin Henderson, cousin of Willy. He is older

than the others and at the time at which this photograph was taken had already had two girlfriends. Both had given him up on the grounds that his clothes were too dirty and shabby. He said that he didn't care: "Lassies are a waste of time," he said. "Everybody kens that. A complete waste of time."

Martin's father beat him regularly. It started after his father was released from Barlinnie Prison, where he served a two-year sentence for a botched robbery. He and his friend Tam Connor attempted to rob a post office but were beaten off by the customers. Fleeing down the street, they found themselves running straight into the arms of the police. The sheriff who sentenced them expressed surprise at their stupidity. "You are very inept," he said. "Very."

Martin hated his father and told his mother that he wanted him dead.

"He's not your faither," she said. "I've been meaning to tell you."

He looked at her. "So you had other men?"

She shrugged. "Everybody did. And don't come over all moral with me, young man. You don't know what it's like."

On certain nights at the local ballroom, it was considered permissible for married women to meet other men. On such nights, groups of women would accompany their friends to the ballroom, where they would be bought drinks by the various predatory men who frequented the bar.

"So who's my faither, then?" asked Martin.

"He was a better class of man than him," replied his mother, nodding in the direction of her husband.

"What was his name?" asked Martin.

"It doesnae matter."

"It does tae me."

She sighed. "All right. Your faither is a man who played the accordion in a ceilidh band. He was called Ross and he came from Mull. He was a kind man."

He stared at her. "You should have told me. You could easily have told me that."

She wondered what good it would have done. "You wouldn't have seen much of him," she said. "We needed somebody right here—somebody who could pay the bills—not somebody who didn't even know he was your faither."

"I might have wanted to meet him."

"What for? What's the point?"

Martin did not press the matter. But years later, when he was seventeen, he defended himself against the man who said he was his father. On that occasion he knocked him to the ground and straddled him. He resisted the temptation to strike at his head and simply pinioned his arms so that he could not unseat him.

"I hate you," he said. "You're a bully."

His father—he still called him that—met his gaze. "You know something?" he said. "Your real faither is a tout—an informer. You know that? The polis use him. We all ken that."

Martin rose to his feet. "You don't know what you're talking about. Your head's full o' mince."

"That's what you think," said his father. "But it's your heid that's full of mince."

Martin had a job in a bakery, but lost it when the baker went bankrupt. He then worked for a while in a hotel in the West End of Glasgow, until he was dismissed for stealing tips from the staff tip boxes.

"That was an utterly despicable thing to do," scolded one of the bar-room staff.

"Shut it," muttered Martin.

 These are Martin's shoes. There is something slightly feminine about these boots—perhaps because of their built-up heels. The effect was to give Martin a slight sense of superiority. He had little time for these kids, with their shabby footwear. His boots had high heels that gave him a good inch and a half extra.

In 1974, Martin killed Johnny Soutar. It happened in a pub that was popular with stock car racers. There was an argument—some witnesses said it was over football, others were not so sure. Johnny Soutar laughed at Martin and said that the football team he supported was never going to get anywhere. Martin, who had taken drink, swung a fist at Johnny, knocking him to the floor. Johnny's head hit the corner of the bar and he never recovered consciousness. It was generally accepted that Martin did not intend to kill Johnny, but that was what he did. Some of the witnesses affirmed that Johnny provoked Martin; others thought that Martin was the aggressor.

Martin was tried for culpable homicide. The judge told the jury that the confusion as to exactly what had happened made it very important that they should deliberate on their verdict very carefully. He clearly thought that Johnny's death was an accident.

Martin was convicted and sentenced to three years in prison. In his car on the way back to Edinburgh, the judge sat quite silently. He thought he had just passed a sentence for what was not much more than an unfortunate accident. He hated that. He hated everything that had made Martin's life such a narrow and deprived one. He knew he could not change anything—that people suffered because they had to. He knew that in a life of privation and violence there would rarely be any room for joy. This narrow, sad life—which he had just made even sadder—would simply have to be endured by Martin Henderson.

"I dislike my job," muttered the judge to himself, gazing out of the car window.

His driver glanced in the rear-view mirror. He had driven judges for years. They had a difficult job, but so did plenty of other people. And he, Norrie Burns, knew just how difficult it was for them to forget the things they had to do.

St. John's Wort

J EAN DEARLY LOVED HER HUSBAND, Brian, but was dis-
tressed by his worrying.

"I know it's a good idea to be aware of risks," she said. "I
know that. And I would never court disaster, but there have
to be limits, don't there? You can't wrap yourself in cotton
wool your whole life, can you?"

"You can't," said her friend Hen. "You'd never get out of
the house if you started to worry about all the things that
might happen to you. *Might,* mind you. A lot of the things
that *could* happen never *will* happen because . . . well, because
they are very unlikely to happen."

"Exactly," said Jean. "We could be hit by a meteorite at any
moment, we're told. There might be one coming towards us
right now—even as we stand here and speak about it. You
can't see them during the day, you know. They could be coming right for you and you wouldn't know."

Hen looked up anxiously. "You mean, there's no warning?
They're just there, flying towards us?"

Jean nodded. "That's what happened to the dinosaurs, apparently. A very large meteorite hit the earth and sent us a
giant cloud of dust. It blocked the warmth of the sun and the
dinosaurs became extinct."

Hen shuddered. "Heavens. And the same thing could happen to us?"

Jean nodded. "Yes, except it probably won't—at least not

while you and I are still alive, Hen. We're unlikely to become extinct."

"That's a relief," said Hen. She paused. "Is that what your man's worried about? Becoming extinct?"

"Oh, he's worried about that in the past. It's always one thing or another—now it's Cuba."

Hen frowned. "Cuba? That place over there . . ." She waved vaguely towards the horizon.

"I think it's more in that direction," said Jean, pointing elsewhere. "But it doesn't matter too much where it is—the point is that there's a lot of trouble brewing over there. Have you listened to the news? Have you heard about it on the wireless?"

Hen shook her head. "Our radio's broken," she said. "The lights still go on when you switch it on, but there's no sound. It's the valves, I think. My Archie knows a bit about radios, and he says when a valve goes you're in trouble."

"It sounds like an old radio," said Jean. "Valves are on the way out, I'm told."

"What will they think of next?" said Hen. "No valves in a radio! Well, that makes you think."

Jean smiled. She had always found her friend to be other-worldly. She had not heard about what was going on in Cuba, and probably barely knew where it was. And here she was in 1962 still talking about the valves in radios.

"Cuba," she said. "It's one of these Communist places, you know. There's a certain Mr. Castro . . ."

"Nice name," interjected Hen.

"Fidel Castro in full."

"Very nice," said Hen.

"Big black beard. Great head of hair. Very revolutionary type."

Hen's eyes widened. "Revolutionary? Like that fellow . . ." She looked for assistance.

"Marx? Yes, but different. Younger. More of a film star than Marx."

Hen frowned. "He's been making trouble then—this Castro?"

"Yes," replied Jean. "A lot of trouble. Him and the Russians. They've sent over a lot of their rockets—you know, the ones with bombs at the end. Atomic bombs."

"You don't want those," said Hen.

"No, you don't. And so the Americans have been getting into a real spin over it. Their President . . ."

"Eisenhower?"

"No, it's Kennedy now."

Hen remembered. "Yes, of course. Him. He's not too pleased about this Castro having all those atomic bombs?"

"He certainly isn't. He's told old Khrushchev that if he doesn't remove them, then he's going to send in the U.S. Navy or something like that. And Khrushchev hasn't been too pleased with being threatened like that, and so it's all very worrying."

"And your Brian is worried about that?"

Jean sighed. "Everybody should be worried—at least a little bit worried. But Brian—well, you know how he is. There we are, living in the back of beyond, and about as far away from everything as you can get, and Brian is sitting there fretting and pacing about and listening to the news every hour. Even at night, he listens. He gets foreign stations on the long wave and listens to what they're saying about it all. It's really getting on top of me, Hen."

Living in the back of beyond. That was Brian's choice. Before they moved to the semi-detached farm cottage they had found advertised in their local paper, they had lived for years on the edge of a small town in a prosperous farming area. Brian was a tractor mechanic who had set up his own business selling and servicing John Deere tractors. This had prospered because of his reliability and competence in tractor matters. "I understand what a tractor is trying to tell me," he said. "If you listen, a tractor will tell you what the problem is."

Shortly after his fifty-seventh birthday, a competing firm, much larger and more aggressive in its sales techniques, had made an offer for Brian's business. The terms seemed absurdly generous, and at first Brian had imagined that a mistake had been made in the noting down of the offer. But it had not: the details set out in the letter of offer were exactly those that the prospective purchasers intended. Brian accepted, and he and Jean decided to move to the country. It was at this point that Brian's growing anxiety came to the surface.

"We need to find somewhere really remote," he said. "It'll be safer."

Jean looked at him in puzzlement. "Safer from what?"

Brian looked over his shoulder. "From threats," he said. "Safer from threats of . . . of all sorts, really. The way this country's going, soon we'll all have to be able to take care of ourselves. It would be much safer to get out into the country, really far from everything, and sit it out there."

"Sit what out?" asked Jean.

Brian lowered his voice. "The coming crisis. The disaster."

"Are you sure there's going to be one?" she asked. "Other people don't seem to be too concerned about things."

"Hah!" said Brian. "There you have it. Foolishness. Lack of a plan. Those people will find out, all right."

They found a remote cottage, one half of which was on the market for very little. Jean did not like it very much: it was several miles from the nearest village, and although it had electricity, there was no telephone line. "We don't need a tele-phone," said Brian. "We don't need to phone anybody."

Behind the cottage was a line of trees—Scots pine, syc-amore, and oak. Ravens nested in some of these trees, and could be heard throughout the day squabbling over the sort of territorial issues that birds like to squabble over. In front of the cottage, whin bushes marched off in disorder towards the narrow road that led to the village. In flower, the whin scented the air, while the sky, which was wide and open, seemed to smell of the rich Lanarkshire farming land that stretched out in all directions. That was a smell of dark soil, and cattle, and freshly mown hay.

But into this quiet Scottish fastness came the news of impending disaster. In the fields of America it was the tips of missiles that bristled, not ears of wheat. And from the east, from behind that rigid curtain, came truculence tinged with fear. At sea, somewhere otherwise blue and distant, rival warships tracked each other's movements, their torpedoes primed.

"Oh, Jeanie," said Brian. "I'm so afraid. I'm so afraid. This is going to end in disaster."

"Good sense will prevail," said Jean, trying to reassure him. "It always does."

But Brian was not convinced. In the middle of the whin bushes there was a disused well. This had run dry years ago when the water table had altered. Now he spent hours down there, investigating it with his flashlight and constructing a system of ladders that led down into the shaft below.

"What are you doing down there, Brian?" Jean asked.

"I'm building a shelter, Jeanie," he replied. "For you and me, and for any other folk who come and ask for admission. I don't want to turn anybody away, as long as we don't get too many."

The construction of the shelter involved excavation, and in this task Jean was called upon to assist. Here, in this photograph, taken by their neighbour Queenie, the widow of a farm grieve, we see Jean sending down the bucket for a further load of earth. Brian is twenty feet below, scraping away at a tunnel that was planned to lead into a large central chamber, lit by twelve-volt tractor batteries.

At the end of the day's work, Brian would listen to the news. It was not good. The two super-powers, armed with sufficient weaponry to do the work of several hundreds of dinosaur-extinguishing meteors, faced one another in grim hostility. These reports made Brian shake his head further and remark on how he would have to speed up his efforts the following day.

Then Queenie said to Jean, "Your man seems a bit low, Jean. A bit down in the dumps."

"Yes," said Jean. "He is. He worries away at things. Mostly Cuba at the moment, but it'll be something else in time."

Queenie looked thoughtful. "Have you tried St. John's wort?" she asked. "It's great for depression."

Jean looked doubtful. "I don't think he'll take anything," she said.

Queenie brushed this aside. "Oh, men often won't take things," she said. "All you have to do is put it in their tea. Works every time."

"You don't have any, do you?" asked Jean.

Queenie did have some. "I'll show you how to use it," she said. "And I'd give your man a muckle great dose, if I were you. He's got a gae storm of worries flying away in that heid of his."

It took a few days for the St. John's wort to work. But then, quite suddenly, Brian announced over breakfast, "I don't think I'll bother with the shelter today."

Jean held her breath. "No?"

"No. I think they'll sort something out over there. They don't want to blow each other to pieces."

"No, they probably don't."

She waited.

"And I thought you and I might go out tonight."

Jean struggled to conceal her astonishment. "Out?"

"Yes. We could go into Glasgow and see a film. Maybe stay overnight at Maggie's." Maggie was his sister, who lived off the Dumbarton Road.

"I'd love that," she said.

And then she said, "Let me give you another cup of tea, Brian."

He smiled at her. "Very good stuff, that."

She caught her breath. She had never lied to him—not once, in all their years of marriage. "That . . ."

"Tea," he said.

Blackmail

T HE GOOD THING about this job," said Nell, "is that you're right at the bottom of the heap. After this, you can't exactly fall any lower." She leaned on her broom and pointed at the gutter. "Yes, we're there already. That's the great thing about being a street sweeper."

Harry agreed with her, and he was amused by her cheerfulness. He had been in the job for little more than a week, and had yet to accustom himself to the fall that had brought him to such a lowly occupation.

Nell had sensed this. "I can tell that you're embarrassed by your position, Harry," she said, fixing him with an intense stare. "No need to be, you know." She paused. "What were you before . . ."

Before my fall, he thought. *Before that fateful day . . .*

"I was in a pretty good job," he said. "I had security and a good wage."

"Oh, we all were," said Nell. "I was a bus conductress. That's a good job, you know. But the public can be trying, and I'm afraid I lost my temper and hit a passenger. There was an awful fuss over it. He was the Chairman of the local Water Board. I lost my job as a result and could get no reference for another one. That's my story."

She looked at him expectantly. He shifted his feet.

"I was the chief financial clerk of a trading firm," Harry said. "We imported timber. I handled all the incoming receipts."

Nell gave him a wary look. "And?"

"And I . . . well, I got into debt. The usual story. I borrowed some of the firm's money, fully intending to pay it back. There was a spot check and the figures didn't add up." He looked away, ashamed at the memory, the humiliation.

"So that was it?"

He nodded. "Yes, that was it. They were kind to me, though. They didn't report it to the police and let me resign. Like you, though, I got no reference and couldn't find anything else without a previous employer to vouch for me. And so here I am . . ."

Nell smiled. "And now you regret what you did?"

He did. "Oh yes, I regret it, all right. I can't pay it back, but I hope one day I'll be able to do something that makes up for it, if you see what I mean."

She understood. "I regret hitting the Chairman of the Water Board," she said. "He was smaller than me—a little mouse of a man, and it was bullying on my part. I think of it a lot." She leaned on her broom and laughed. "So here we are, two lost souls, wanting to make up for something we did." She looked thoughtful. "It's odd, isn't it, how a single mistake can change the whole course of a life. One foot wrong and the next thing you know is you're sweeping the streets."

"Yes, I've often thought that too. It's very odd."

Nell leaned on her brush again. "Almost unfair."

"Yes, you could say that."

Nell looked up. "Of course, you do realise that this job has its compensations."

He waited for her to expand.

"Human interest is one of them," she said. "This is one of the most interesting jobs there is."

He felt inclined to laugh. "What? Sweeping the streets? I'm sorry, I can't see that."

Nell raised an eyebrow. "That might be because you haven't opened your eyes to it. A lot of people don't notice the interesting things around them. They go through life thinking everything's very dull, and all the time it's the opposite." She stared at him. "You don't believe me, do you?"

"Well, no, not really."

"All right," she said. "Let me spell it out for you. While you're sweeping the streets . . ." She moved her brush along the gutter. "Sweeping like this, see. While you're doing that, people are passing you by. They're talking. You hear what they have to say—little snippets, mostly, but full of human interest. You know what I heard a man say yesterday?"

"No."

"I heard him say, 'I've decided to shoot him. I've had enough—I really have.'"

Harry looked alarmed. "You heard that? Right here?"

"Over there," said Nell, pointing to the other side of the street. "I was working on a pile of leaves that was blocking a drain and I heard these two men talking. One of them said that—those very words."

"Did you go to the police?"

Nell laughed. "Oh no, that wasn't necessary. One of them, you see, is a racehorse trainer. I know that because I see him with the racing paper tucked under his arm when he leaves his house in the morning. And Bert, who sells the papers, told me that he was a trainer. He was talking about a horse, you see. That's not a police matter."

Harry shook his head. "Poor horse. He's obviously playing up, but shooting's a bit extreme."

"Oh, he won't do it. I spoke to Bert about it, and he says he's just using it as a figure of speech. They'll take him off the track and use him for something else."

"I'm relieved to hear that," said Harry.

"And then," Nell continued, "I picked up a very amusing snippet. Laughed for a day, I did, as did my Joe when I told him about it. I came round the corner one day and there were two women standing on the pavement saying goodbye to one another. And the one said to the other, 'Send me a postcard when the baby can say *banana*.'"

Harry chuckled. "Well, well . . ."

"Joe and I often say that when we take leave of one another. *Send me a postcard when the baby can say* banana."

She looked above the chemist's shop further down the street. "We'd better get on with the job," she said. "They're not paying us to talk."

They worked together for fifteen minutes, finding that the swing of their brushes seemed to synchronise. It was companionable work, thought Harry, and considerably less stressful than being a chief financial clerk.

They reached a lamp-post on the edge of a square, and Nell stopped. "Five minutes' break," she said. She lowered her voice. "Don't make it too obvious, but look over there."

Harry followed her gaze. A tall, well-built man wearing a bowler hat was in conversation with a smaller, rather weasel-like man standing in front of him. The conversation was an animated one.

Her voice lowered, Nell continued, "The gentleman in the bowler is called Eustace Potter. Billy, the waiter in the café over there, told me that."

Harry glanced at the café further along the square. A large Schweppes sign advertised its presence.

"It's a great place for people to meet, that café. They go there to meet their friends, but often it's their lovers, you know."

Harry's eyes widened. "Assignations?"

"If that's what you want to call them." Nell snorted. "Yes, and that fellow, Potter, meets a young woman there every other day. I've seen them when I've been sweeping outside. Very lovey-dovey. And then one day—last Tuesday, I think it was—in he comes with a different woman. And I think to myself, *Now then, Nell, she looks like a different cup of tea altogether.* And she is, of course. She's his wife."

Harry was following this with interest. "And the man he's talking to?"

"That," explained Nell, "is one Norman Frye. He frequents that café too—oh yes, he does. Right regular is our Mr. Frye."

"Meeting somebody as well?"

Nell shook her head. "No. He's there for professional reasons. Mr. Frye, you see, is a blackmailer. That's what he does.

He sees these men meeting their mistresses and he writes it all down. Noses about a bit. Then he threatens to disclose it all to their wives unless the husbands pay what he's asking. And his silence doesn't come cheaply, I'm told."

Harry let out a whistle. "You really know your patch," he said.

Nell looked proud. "I keep my eyes open." She pointed towards the two men in conversation. "I can tell you what's going on there. Norman Frye has spotted Potter's wife on the other side of the square. You see her? She's coming over to talk to her husband.

"Now Norman Frye has seen his opportunity. He'll be saying to Potter that unless he pays him a certain sum  immediately—on the spot— he, Norman Frye, is going to have something to say to his wife. And that will be all about the meetings that her Eustace has in the café with a certain young woman." Nell gripped Harry's arm. "Look. See what's happening. Potter's reaching into his pocket and . . . yes, that's money that's being paid over. See it?"

Harry felt the back of his neck getting warm with indignation. Apart from one little incident of unauthorised borrowing—and he had intended it to be borrowing—he was an honest man. Blackmail, the crime that they had just witnessed, was something quite different. It was despicable. It involved fear. It involved taking advantage of the weakness of others. It was a loathsome way of earning a living—far worse than embezzlement or even armed robbery.

They watched as Norman Frye slipped away, retreating into the café. They continued to watch as Eustace Potter greeted his wife, who had now arrived from the other side of the square.

"Butter wouldn't melt in his mouth," said Nell. "Hypocrite!" She paused. "But then most men are hypocrites . . . if you don't mind my saying that, Harry. No offence, of course."

"None taken," Harry assured her.

"Let's get on," said Nell. "Break over."

They continued with their sweeping. A few minutes later, they were outside the café, able to look in from the pavement and see what was happening within. There was Norman Frye, seated at a table at the far end, reading a newspaper, evidently pleased with his morning's work. And there were the Potters, nearer the window. Mrs. Potter had obviously insisted on their going inside for tea, as her husband looked distinctly uncomfortable and was stealing the occasional glance at his blackmailer on the other side of the room.

Suddenly Harry had an idea. "Come inside with me," he whispered to Nell.

"What are you planning?" she asked. "We don't belong in there."

"Just come," said Harry. "You'll see."

Harry walked through the café to the table where Norman Frye was seated. "Norman Frye?" he asked.

Norman Frye lowered his newspaper. "Yes."

"Detective Constable Harold Duffy," he said. "Plain Clothes Department. Blackmail squad. And this"—he gestured towards Nell—"is Woman Detective Constable Nellie Evans. We've been watching you, Mr. Frye."

Norman Frye's face drained of all colour. He opened his mouth to speak, but no sound came.

Harry leaned forward. "However, you're a very lucky villain, Mr. Frye—a very lucky one."

Norman Frye stared up in terror.

"Because," Harry continued, "you happen to have come up against not only the most observant coppers in London, but also the most corrupt ones. So, if you'd kindly hand over all the money in your possession—not just the funds you have just extorted from Mr. Eustace Potter, over there, but also the float that I believe you people often carry with you. Hand over the lot and you'll hear no more from us—provided you clear out of this manor and are not seen back here again—ever. Understand?"

It took Norman Frye not much more than a minute to disgorge a considerable amount of money. Then it took no more than a further minute for him to leave the café hurriedly, his coat collar pulled up to hide his evident fear.

Harry turned around and walked over to the table where the Potters were seated.

"Mr. Potter," he said.

Eustace Potter looked up. "Yes?"

"I'm from the bookmakers, sir," Harry said. "That little wager you placed with us the other day—the horse romped home. You forgot to collect your winnings. So here they are."

Eustace Potter looked at Harry with utter incomprehension as a thick wad of banknotes was placed before him. "The bet you placed in the street back there with our Mr. Frye," Harry continued. "Mr. Frye. Remember?"

"Oh yes," stuttered Eustace Potter. "That. Of course."

Harry straightened up and nodded to Mrs. Potter. "Your husband has a fine eye for the horses," he said. "Good day, Mrs. Potter."

They left the café.

"Well!" exclaimed Nell.

"I needed to do that," said Harry. "Remember what I said about making up for things. This job obviously has possibilities, don't you think?"

"Well!" repeated Nell.

They went back into the street. Both were smiling.

"I must be on my way," said Harry. And then he added, "Send me a postcard when the baby can say *banana*."

Pogo Sticks and
Man with Bicycle

THEY BOUGHT HIM volumes of *The Children's Encyclopaedia*. He loved them. A subscription cost five shillings, but look what it gave you: *how things work; the march of mankind from barbarism to the League of Nations; the wonders of the Ancient World; the waterways of France; how Mr. Bernoulli solved the problem of flight; magnetism explained.* And so much else, in volume after red-bound volume, with the name of Arthur Mee, the encyclopaedia's tireless compiler, prominently embossed on the cover.

Each volume arrived at an interval determined by Mr. Mee, and addressed to: *Master Francis Crick*. The sight of his name on the packaging filled him with pride. *Master Francis Crick*—that's me, he thought. Me.

He lay on his bed and read the encyclopaedias from cover to cover.

"You can't read all night," said his mother. "You'll ruin your eyesight, for one thing. And for another, a growing boy needs sleep."

Why we need to sleep was in fact the title of one of the articles. It seemed that scientists agreed with his mother: we needed to sleep.

She came into his room at night and took the heavy volume off his chest, where it had dropped when he dozed off. She switched off the light and lingered, watching him fondly—her flesh and blood, whom she had made, fashioned from cells within her own body, hers. What words were there to make known that pride, that love? Or were these best expressed in a look, that look a mother gives her son when she finds him asleep, an opened volume of Arthur Mee's *Children's Encyclopaedia* beside him on the bed?

He went first to the science articles.

"I think I'm going to be a scientist when I grow up," he said. "In a laboratory."

"Good," said his father. "We need boffins."

The war came. The Government said, "We need boffins," and Francis Crick, now a graduate of University College, London, joined the Admiralty. He was put to work designing mines that would attach themselves magnetically to ships. He knew the work was important, but he did not want to spend the rest of his life designing arms. He went to Cambridge and started to work in the Cavendish Laboratory on the structure of proteins.

He met James Watson, an American scientist who was twelve years his junior. They worked together in Cambridge, exploring the way in which the nature of DNA might be understood. They attempted to build a model of the acid, but its shape eluded them.

"Frustration squared," growled Crick. "The crystallography data's there, so why can't we get it to stack up?"

"Maybe we can't," said Watson.

"No such word. Not in science."

"All right," said Watson. "Maybe *won't*. *Won't* and *can't* are different concepts. *Won't* is predictive of what might happen; *can't* is expressive of a limitation that we *know* is there."

"I'd probably agree with that," said Crick.

Two of the undergraduates, assisting one of the professors in a lab project, had brought with them that day two pogo sticks. Crick was intrigued.

"You use these for jumping?"

The undergraduates smiled. "It's just a bit of fun," said one. "An alternative means of self-propulsion."

"The principle is obvious," said Watson. "Force transferred back in the exact opposite direction from that in which it comes. Classic."

"Yes," said Crick, smiling. "Chap's weight applies force through spring in direction of ground. Force meets resistance from ground and is transmitted back, through spring, to send chap back up."

"What a bouncing ball does," offered one of the students.

Watson said, "Could you show us?"

"What—here in the lab?" asked the other student. "We'd break something."

"Outside, then," said Watson. "You coming to see this, Crick?"

"I'll bring my camera," Crick said.

They went outside—the two scientists, and the two students, who were called Evans and Prender. Crick was always confusing them, calling Evans Prender and Prender Evans. They had first names, of course, but he had forgotten what those were. He thought that Evans might be called Tommy, but then he realised that he had once known a Tommy Evans in the Ministry during the war and he might be thinking of him. That Tommy Evans worked on torpedoes and was a formidable chess player. He lived in Maida Vale with a Turkish woman called . . . Crick could not quite remember. He had once called her Mrs. Evans, which she was not, and she had beamed with pleasure at the compliment. "You really should marry that woman of yours," he had said to Evans. But Evans had simply shaken his head and said, "Good God, no. Not that."

Passers-by watched with amusement as Evans and Prender prepared to use the pogo sticks.

"You know, they invented these things back in the late nineties," said Evans (or possibly Prender).

"A big step," commented Watson. "Or bounce, rather."

"Hah," said Crick.

They started to bounce up and down. Both had clearly mastered the art of staying upright on a pogo stick, although Prender seemed a bit better at it than Evans. He was also less inhibited, emitting shouts of excitement and encouragement to his friend.

Two women, walking behind them, smiled at the sight of the undergraduate high spirits.

"These boys," said Sylvie Manners to her friend. "Look at them—not a care in the world. Not a care."

"They say the proctors have a terrible job keeping them in order," said the friend. "These night climbers, for instance."

"Oh, them. Well, I'm surprised they're still alive—half of them. Did you hear that one of them put an umbrella on top of the lightning conductor at John's? At the very top? What if he'd fallen?"

"Certain death," said the friend, grimly. "But then, at their age you're immortal, aren't you? Death is something that happens to somebody else, not you."

The young men's antics were observed by somebody else. Pushing his bicycle up the same pedestrian alley, glancing discreetly at the display, was a man of thirty-two, who felt the cold terribly and was well wrapped up in his heavy twill overcoat. He was Mr. James da Silva, a scholar of English literature from Cochin, in the Indian state of Kerala. James da Silva was the son of Matthew da Silva and his wife, Kitty. Matthew was the owner of a pharmacy in Cochin, Da Silva's First Class Pharmacy, and of a small pepper estate in the Western Ghats, the range of hills that rose in the Cochin hinterland. The pepper estate was run by Kitty's parents, who had lost their own business through the depredations of a dishonest book-keeper. Matthew came to their rescue, allowing them to occupy the main house on the pepper estate, and to derive a small income from the sale of the crop. "You've saved my parents' lives," said Kitty. "You're a good man, Matthew."

Until 1896 the da Silva family had been Hindu, but had been converted in that year by a missionary from Bristol. Now they were members of the Church of South India, a loosely Anglican denomination, although James had sympathies for at least some of the Hindu pantheon, especially Ganesh. The elephant-headed god seemed to him to be so reassuring, less stern, perhaps, than some of the Christian saints, and less judgemental, as were all the Hindu deities. As a boy, he kept a small Ganesh figure, carved in soft stone, in a drawer in his room. His mother would not have approved; for her eyes, a picture of the Blessed Virgin was displayed on the shelf above his bed, portrayed as she had appeared to Tamil Krishnannesti Sankaranarayanan on the road to Nagapattinam. He thought that the Virgin would have been at ease in the company of Ganesh, were they ever to meet, and it did not help, he felt, for the followers of one to deny to the followers of the other that their object of devotion ever existed, or was false.

James was the cleverest boy in his school. That was the judgement of the school principal, who helped him win a prestigious scholarship to the University of Bombay. Now here he was in Cambridge, studying for an advanced degree, writing a thesis on the novels of Trollope. He had arrived the week before, and the October weather had chilled him to the bone. He knew that England would be cold—everybody had warned him of this—but he had not expected this relentless wind that seemed to come sweeping in from somewhere far away, Russia perhaps, which was even colder, they said.

And it was all so odd—so familiar, and yet so foreign. He had known plenty of Englishmen in Bombay—there were still professors at the university, who were staying on after the hand-over—and his father knew some pharmacists and doctors who seemed not to have noticed that the Raj had officially packed up, or did not mind, perhaps. But they seemed very different from the people he was meeting here in Cambridge, who seemed so much less interested in the world, so much more buried away in their cold and draughty homes. Englishmen in India belonged to clubs and played tennis. Where were the clubs and tennis courts here?

And these young men with their strange devices, jumping up and down like children. These were not boys of the sort you would find in any village in India, entertaining themselves with stilts and the like—these were young men, in their twenties, it seemed to him, and they were playing with *toys* on the public street. What were they thinking of? He averted his gaze. He felt suddenly homesick for Cochin and for an England that he dreamed of and that now he thought might not exist any longer.

The demonstration over, and Crick having photographed Evans and Prender on their pogo sticks, the four of them returned to the laboratory. Crick asked Prender to show him one of the pogo sticks.

"Remarkable things," he said. "Quite sturdy, I should imagine—to take your weight."

"Yes," said Prender. "The works are down there at the bottom—obviously. There's a very tough spring."

Crick examined the pogo stick. It was possible, he noticed, to unscrew the barrel of the stick at that point to expose the spring within.

"Quite a device," Crick said. "Look at it. A sort of double helix."

Watson looked up sharply. "What?" he asked.

"A double helix," said Crick, pointing to the spring inserted in the base of the pogo stick.

Watson stared at Crick. Crick stared back at Watson.

In the street, James da Silva parked his bicycle outside a tearoom and went inside to order a pot of tea. The woman behind the counter smiled at him, and for a short time he felt rather better.

La Plage

A ND MADELEINE SAID TO HIM, as they walked along the beach, on the raked sand, "Mother never liked that young woman, you know—the one who became engaged to Henri. Remember her?"

He was looking over to the left, towards the bathing machines, which seemed to him to be like the war devices of an invading army, bright besiegers with their flags and devices, like Greeks lined up against Troy. And there amongst all those people, he thought, were Achilles and Patroclus and all the others. And the sea, which Homer always described as wine-dark, but which was so different here in Normandy.

She continued, "Mother was right, you know. It's an odd thing, isn't it: you never want your mother to be right, but the older you get, the more right you realise your mother was. All those things that mothers say, all those annoying things, turn out to be right."

He thought: Oh yes? Did I ever listen to anything my mother said? Not really. Do I listen to anything that any women say to me? They're always addressing me, it seems—all the time. Which is kind of them, I suppose, and I should pay more attention, I know I should, but . . .

"You see," she went on, "I know Henri is my brother and that means I'm biased. Of course I am. I did try, you know; I tried my best to be positive towards her, right from the time he first brought her back to the house. That must have been, what? Almost a year ago? Was it June, do you think? June, or possibly July?"

He thought it was June, but he did not say as much. What did it matter? June was pretty much the same as July, when you came to think about it. And when you looked back, from the vantage point of September, when he would sometimes go fishing with his friend Alphonse, who was bankrupt now— poor Alphonse! That investment that I should have warned him against because I had read somewhere about how those plantations were susceptible to bad weather—to hurricanes, even—I should have persuaded him to leave his money in the bank. I should have.

"It was June," she said. "I remember that because it was shortly after the *curé*'s horse died. He made such a fuss about that, although the horse was twenty-eight, at least, and that's quite an age for a horse. Anyway, it was after that, because the *curé* had been round at the house and going on and on about his wretched horse, and we had to sit there and listen because Mother wouldn't drop one of her hints for him to go. Remember how she tried to get rid of the mayor once by looking at the sky and saying it was going to rain and he should hurry up and go home if he wanted to avoid being soaked to the skin? And the sky was cloudless—absolutely not a cloud to be seen—and rain was the very last thing that anybody was expecting. Remember that? And the mayor looked out of the window and said, 'But, Madame de Villiers, the weather is remarkably fine,' and Mother said, *'Au contraire . . .'* She was always saying *au contraire* when she didn't have a leg to stand on, and she said, *'Au contraire,*

M. le Maire, there is every chance that there will be rain—and heavy rain at that. I would not want to be responsible for you catching pneumonia.' You'd have thought he would take the hint, but sometimes these people—well, you know what they're like. It would take a bomb to shift them from their seat once you've served them their tea and there are still some cakes and sandwiches on the plate."

He gazed over at the bathing machines. He knew a man who had bought four of them, as an investment, or so he told people. But all along this man had been a deviant who had drilled small holes in the back of the bathing machines so that he could watch people inside when they changed into their bathing costumes. He pretended to be maintaining the machines, but all the time he was peeping in from the back. What an absurd thing to do! How desperate must one be to do a thing like that. That man was never caught—not by the authorities—although some husband found him out. He saw an eye staring in through a hole in the woodwork and poked at it with the tip of his walking stick. The man was lucky not to lose his eye; he had a bad bruise, but he deserved it. He could have been in even deeper trouble. That's the thing about trouble, of course: no matter what trouble you're in, there's always deeper trouble around the corner. It's a good thing to remember that when you're feeling sorry for yourself.

"No, it was definitely June, and Henri rather sprung it on Mother. He asked her whether he could bring somebody round for lunch on Sunday, and she thought it was one of his friends. Somebody like that fellow Charles—you remember him? The one who was so greedy when he came to lunch, had three helpings of everything—three!—and talked about a German motor car that his father had recently bought that had two reverse gears? Do you remember that? I sat there thinking, *Why would anybody need two reverse gears?* And I still don't have an answer to that. I suppose Charles has his good points, and he did make a very good marriage eventually— not that he invited us to the wedding. You'd think after all the food that he'd eaten in our house he would have the decency to reciprocate, but no. She came from Lyons, apparently—his new wife—and she had inherited a small fortune from some uncle or other. Charles bought a chateau on the Loire—not one of these big ones, it wasn't Villandry by any means, but quite a nice place nonetheless. He had a bit of land as well, along the river, and he had some tenants who were troglo- dytes. Those cliffs along the river lend themselves to that sort of thing. Those houses carved into the cliffs can be quite com- fortable, they tell me. Cold in summer and warm enough in the winter. I suppose you don't get any draughts, really, and that must make a difference."

He thought, But darkness would be the issue for a trog- lodyte. The rooms in the front would have natural light, but everything behind that would be pitch dark. You would need to have the lights on all the time, and even then it would be a bit dim. Would he like it? It would be a good place to keep wine. It would, in fact, be like living in a wine cellar, which some people would like, he supposed. Some bibulous individuals.

"I knew something was up," she said. "I knew that Henri was planning to bring somebody special, because he spent hours in the bathroom that morning, before he went off to collect her. Hours. And when I went in, there were all those pomades he puts on his hair—you know, that sandalwood stuff, and the wax that he uses for his moustache—and his eyebrows too. Did you know that Henri puts wax on his eyebrows? He does, you know. Wax. And so I knew that he was going to spring something on us, and I was right.

"I always remember the way she came into the drawing room and looked around, as if to pass judgement on it. You don't do that, Paul, you just don't. You don't go into somebody else's drawing room and look around as if you're an auctioneer come to appraise the furniture. And then she brushed the seat of the chair before she sat down—actually brushed it—as if we would have dirty upholstery. What an insult! It was nothing less than an insult.

"And I realised pretty much straight away that she was illiterate. Because I said to her something about Montaigne, and, you know, she looked absolutely blank. Face as flat as a pancake. All I said was something like, 'Montaigne would agree, would he not?' And she stared at me. Then, a little bit later, I mentioned Proust, and again no reaction. To Proust! No reaction when half of Paris is talking about Proust. You'd think that she would have a view on him, even if she hadn't read a word he's written, but no, not a flicker of an eyelid.

"Poor Henri, he was doing his best. He said, 'Annette is very interested in the theatre.' He was trying to impress us, to make up for her only-too-evident ignorance of Montaigne and Proust. So I said, helpfully, I thought, 'What plays have you seen recently?' and she opened her mouth and not a syllable came out. Not one. So Mother, bless her, said, 'My good-ness, it looks like rain again,' but of course it was another completely cloudless day."

He stared at the people on the beach. None of them was in a bathing outfit. Nobody. Even the children were fully dressed. They were sitting about on the beach, some on chairs, some on the sand itself. Some stood idly, as if waiting for something to happen. And the wind was blowing garments tied to a line, the arms flapping as if signalling something to somebody somewhere else altogether.

He thought: Life is a long road that all of us have to walk along. We don't always know where we're going, but we trudge along it dutifully, for the most part. Of course, you can wander off; you can let go of the arm of the person who walks beside you and you can wander off. I could wander off, over this odd rampart that separates one part of this beach from the other, and I could find myself amongst these people who seem to be waiting for something to happen. But I shall not do that, because my lines in the play require me to be on this stage, rather than that. So you carry on, although every so often you look off to the left, or to the right, and you think about other things and the wind blows and the sand

gets in your eyes, as it can do, and the crowd in the distance mills around the patisseries, as crowds will mill, and the band playing in the bandstand works its way through the bars of music that it is its duty to play all the way to the end and to the silence that comes at the end.

Alexander McCall Smith is the author of the No. 1 Ladies' Detective Agency novels and a number of other series and stand-alone books. His works have been translated into more than forty languages and have been best sellers throughout the world. He lives in Scotland.